OCT 2 0 2017

M DUN

Much Ado About Murder

Also Available by Elizabeth J. Duncan

Shakespeare in the Catskills Mysteries:

Ill Met by Murder

Untimely Death

Penny Brannigan Mysteries:

Murder Is for Keeps

Murder on the Hour

Slated for Death

Never Laugh as a Hearse Goes By

A Small Hill to Die On

A Killer's Christmas in Wales

A Brush With Death

The Cold Light of Mourning

Much Ado About Murder

A Shakespeare in the Catskills Mystery

Elizabeth J. Duncan

CROOKED
LANE

NEW YORK

Copyright © 2017 by copyright Elizabeth J. Duncan

Published in the United States by Crooked Lane Books, an imprint of The Quick Brown Fox & Company LLC.

Crooked Lane Books and its logo are trademarks of The Quick Brown Fox & Company LLC.

Library of Congress Catalog-in-Publication data available upon request.

ISBN (hardcover): 978-1-68331-325-0
ISBN (ePub): 978-1-68331-326-7
ISBN (ePDF): 978-1-68331-328-1

Cover illustration by Ben Perini
Book design by Jennifer Canzone

Printed in the United States.

www.crookedlanebooks.com

Crooked Lane Books
34 West 27th St., 10th Floor
New York, NY 10001

First Edition: November 2017

10 9 8 7 6 5 4 3 2 1

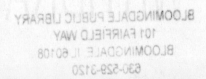

For Sheila Fletcher

Chapter 1

Car arriving now. Charlotte Fairfax read the text out loud to her companion and added, "They're here. Show time."

Paula Van Dusen adjusted the curtains one last time, allowing a wider band of late afternoon sunlight to spill into the sitting room and illuminate the vase of exuberant pink-and-white roses cut from her own garden that she had carefully positioned on the mahogany side table. After ensuring the silver spoons on the tea tray were lined up precisely, she took a deep breath, stepped back, and surveyed the room.

"I hope they like it."

"They'd better," Charlotte replied. "And I can't see why they wouldn't."

The two women, who had spent the afternoon arranging furniture and putting the finishing touches on their redecoration project, closed the door of the star bungalow and fell into step on the path that led to the front entrance of Jacobs Grand Hotel.

"Do you think it was wise to bring Rupert?" Paula Van Dusen asked, referring to the tricolor corgi trotting along between them. "What if she doesn't like dogs?"

"Of course she likes dogs," Charlotte replied. "She's English."

"Well, being English yourself, you should know," replied Paula.

They reached the graveled drop-off area in front of the hotel to find Harvey Jacobs, the hotel's third-generation owner, standing at the top of the white-stuccoed steps. Wearing an old-fashioned three-piece suit, his thumbs tucked in the pockets of the pinstripe vest that strained across his well-upholstered stomach, he shifted his weight from one small foot to the other.

He acknowledged the two women as they took their places on a lower step, and a moment later, a gleaming burgundy Rolls-Royce glided to a slow stop in front of them. The little welcoming party waited while the chauffeur emerged from the driver's seat, opened the rear door closest to them, and stood to one side, touching the visor of his gray cap. A long leg clad in a black stocking and a sleek black pump emerged from the back seat, followed by the other leg and then the rest of an elegant woman. When she was out of the car, the chauffeur ambled around the back of the vehicle and opened the other passenger door for the last occupant, a short woman who wore her gray hair in a trim pageboy style. Her mouth drooped at the corners, accentuated by a sagging jawline, giving her a stern, unintended contemptuous look. She wore dark shapeless trousers and a pale-blue cardigan, with a beige raincoat draped over her left arm. In her right hand, she held a battered brown leather briefcase.

When the new arrivals were standing together beside the car, Paula Van Dusen stepped forward and extended her hand to the first woman. In her early fifties, Paula wore her dark hair pulled back in a tidy chignon. Her complexion was smooth and unlined, and she looked like the kind of woman who could wear red lipstick until the end of her days. She carried herself with an air of confident authority, as if she was used to asking for what she wanted in a way that was polite but firm and always got the result she expected.

"Miss Ashley. Hello. I'm Paula Van Dusen, chairperson of the board of directors of the Catskills Shakespeare Theater Company, and it's my very great pleasure to welcome you. Our cast and crew are so looking forward to working with you."

"Thank you," Audrey Ashley replied in a clipped, precise English accent. "And may I introduce my sister and manager, Maxine Kaminski."

Paula held out her hand to the other woman. "I hope you had a good journey from London. It's a long flight. You must both be exhausted."

"It has been a long day," Audrey Ashley acknowledged, "especially when you factor in the five-hour time difference."

"Of course." Paula Van Dusen gestured to her companion, who took a step forward. "And now I'd like you to meet Charlotte Fairfax, our company's costume designer."

When the women had greeted one another, Paula Van Dusen indicated to the man on the steps that it was his turn to be introduced. "And this is Harvey Jacobs, owner of the hotel."

"Miss Ashley," gushed Harvey, descending the stairs nimbly, considering his weight. "Welcome to Jacobs Grand Hotel. We hope you'll be very happy during your stay here with us." He nodded at her companion. "And you too, of course, Miss, er . . ." His words trailed off and ended in an embarrassed little cough.

"Thank you. That's very kind," Audrey Ashley replied, turning her gaze to the white-frame building behind him. Her head tilted back slightly as her eyes roamed upward over the three stories.

She then directed her wide-set blue-violet eyes to Charlotte's corgi.

"And who's this?" She bent over and gave the dog a friendly pat. Over Audrey's head of frosty-blonde curls, Charlotte threw Paula Van Dusen a rather smug I-told-you-so glance.

"That's Rupert," she said. Rupert waggled his bottom in his usual friendly fashion.

"Oh, what a lovely little fellow." Audrey straightened up. "And now, if you wouldn't mind showing us to our suite, please. I must admit, I am rather starting to fade."

"You'll be staying in our star bungalow," Harvey said. "We'll have your bags delivered in just a few minutes. These ladies will be happy to take you there now and help you get settled in."

"Oh, a bungalow! How charming. Like at the Beverly Hills Hotel, you mean?" she asked, referring to the famous Los Angeles hotel where the grounds were dotted with hillside and poolside bungalows, and the likes of Marilyn Monroe, Elizabeth Taylor, and Richard Burton had partied.

"Yes, well, sort of." Harvey ran a pudgy finger around his sweaty collar. "I guess you could say that."

As Paula, Maxine, and Audrey set off for the bungalow, he hissed to Charlotte, "Have you seen Aaron? He was meant to be here to help with the arrival of the star actress."

"He must be nearby," Charlotte said. "He sent me a text letting me know they'd arrived, and since you're here, you must have got the text from him as well."

"When I get my hands on that boy . . ."

"Never mind that now. You've got to calm down," said Charlotte. "Look, here he comes," she added, tipping her head in the direction of the wooded parkland adjacent to the hotel. "There's no problem, so don't make this into one. Paula's more than capable of looking after Audrey and Maxine for a few minutes."

Slightly out of breath, Aaron lurched to a stop beside Charlotte and his uncle. Aaron was in his early twenties and had a head of dark curly hair and unremarkable but pleasant features. He had studied fashion design at Parsons in New York City but, after interning with Charlotte, had decided to pursue a career in costume design.

"Did you want me to carry the bags to the bungalow?" he asked.

"Yes," said his uncle. "That's the general idea." The chauffeur, who was staring into the trunk of his vehicle, breathed a sigh of relief when Aaron materialized and easily lifted four pieces of matching luggage in a timeless brown pattern and two plain black suitcases out of the car and set them on the gravel.

"Well, if there's nothing else, I'd best get back inside," Harvey said. "No point in hanging 'round here. Nancy's got plenty of things lined up to keep me busy for the rest of the day." He disappeared into the hotel, and Charlotte turned her attention to Paula Van Dusen's chauffeur, Barnes.

Tall and thin, he carried himself with a shoulders-back, no-nonsense posture that hinted at a military background. Although his employer had told him several times he could wear a plain dark suit, he proudly opted to remain in the traditional gray chauffeur's uniform with the double row of gold buttons that started wide at the shoulders and tapered as they descended toward the bottom of the jacket. A small gray mustache clung to his upper lip with the tenacity of an elderly centipede. His eyes were hidden behind dark-green aviator sunglasses.

"Barnes, I don't know how much longer Mrs. Van Dusen will be. So it might be best if you parked around the side of the hotel, and if you go inside to the staff cafeteria, they'll be happy to give you a cup of coffee while you wait for her," Charlotte said.

"A piece of pie wouldn't go amiss. This hotel used to serve the best homemade pies in the Catskills. People came from all over to have a piece of pie and a cup of coffee in the little coffee shop they had." Barnes let out a resigned sigh. "Long gone, of course. But then nothing nowadays is as good as it used to be."

"I'm sure they'll be happy to give you a piece of pie or cake, or whatever they've got," Charlotte assured him.

Barnes climbed back in the car, and as he drove slowly off, Aaron set the two black suitcases beside the stairs, picked up the two brown ones, and with Charlotte in charge of the matching carryall and beauty case, they set off down the path to the star bungalow.

In the hotel's heyday, the three bungalows in the grounds were occupied by vacationing families, but two were now home to members of the Catskills Shakespeare Theater Company: Charlotte and her partner, Ray, lived in one, and the second was included in the contract of the director, currently Simon Dyer. The third, known as the star bungalow, provided on-site accommodation for the season's star performer.

The star performer position was filled by a British actor or actress who still had several seasons of good performances ahead of them but was no longer the box office draw in the United Kingdom they had once been. On this side of the Atlantic, however, with the cachet of a polished

British accent, they had box office clout. The previous star, who had been forced to return home to England for medical treatment, had suggested as his replacement an actress whose long and distinguished career had undergone a huge boost over the past few years when she portrayed a crusty dowager in a popular television costume drama. But concerned about the travel and time away from home, she had declined, recommending a colleague who had played a scheming servant in the same series.

The Catskills Shakespeare Theater Company normally performed three plays per season: two comedies and one tragedy. The spring and summer seasons had seen *Romeo and Juliet*, *King Lear*, and *A Midsummer Night's Dream* in repertoire. However, with the departure of the lead actor, it had been decided that the company would drop all three plays from the fall schedule and replace them with an exclusive run of *Much Ado About Nothing*.

And so, Audrey Ashley had agreed to play the part of Beatrice in *Much Ado*. A seasoned performer in her midforties who had enjoyed great popularity as a child actress, she had transitioned successfully into adult roles, and although she had timed out of playing some of the more youthful of Shakespeare's female roles and was at the outer edge of others, with soft lighting and a well-designed costume, she could still take on many of the best parts. Theater audiences, after all, agree at every performance to suspend disbelief and to believe the unbelievable.

Charlotte knocked on the door of the star bungalow, and a moment later, Paula Van Dusen answered it.

"You can leave the bags just there," Paula Van Dusen instructed Aaron as he and Charlotte entered the kitchen. "Thank you. Charlotte and I can manage from here." Aaron set the suitcases down, and Charlotte indicated he should return to the hotel to fetch the remaining luggage.

Charlotte picked up two large suitcases, carried them through the sitting room, and deposited them in the larger of the two bedrooms. Over the past three weeks, the bungalow had undergone a complete but somewhat unintentional refurbishment, as a bit of freshening up had led to a complete makeover.

Paula Van Dusen had sent workers from Oakland, her magnificent estate located a few miles outside town, to smarten everything up. Old flooring had been ripped up and new carpets and hardwood flooring laid, and a new kitchen and bathroom installed. The property had been painted inside and out, and clean, bright rooms were now filled with new, comfortable furniture.

Fortunately, Paula Van Dusen knew a lot of tradesmen and had called in so many favors that almost all the goods and services had been donated. And she herself had loaned one or two pieces of fine furniture and artwork to dress the sitting room.

Although the work had been done under pressure to ensure the rooms were ready for Audrey's arrival, Paula

Van Dusen had seen to it that the work had been done right.

"You did a great job overseeing this project, Paula," Charlotte said when Paula appeared in the bedroom doorway with the lighter bags. She set them down and crossed to the window.

"It would have been better if we'd had a couple of days to air everything out," Paula said. "The smell of the paint and new carpet is almost overpowering." She unlocked the newly installed window and opened it. It slid easily along in its track, and a warm blast of late summer air drifted in. Charlotte ran a smoothing hand over the new coverlet on the queen-sized bed, and the two women returned to the sitting room.

Having slipped off her shoes, Audrey had settled herself in the sitting room, and thanks to the restorative properties of Earl Grey tea, had perked up a little. The plate of Scottish shortbread biscuits on the tea table remained untouched. Maxine hovered near her, ready to relieve her of the cup and saucer.

"I hope you aren't allergic to paint or carpeting," Paula commented. "That awful chemical smell they give off when they're new really bothers some people. Unfortunately, we were working to a very tight deadline, and there wasn't time to get the place aired out properly." Audrey handed her empty cup to Maxine and sank back into the comfort of the new dove-gray sofa. After lifting her stockinged feet onto the ottoman, she reclined fully, motionless, with her eyes closed.

"The smell is rather noticeable," she said, "but I can live with it. I expect we'll get used to it, and besides, it should go away soon." Her eyes remained closed. They had been expertly made up, with a light touch of blended mauve eye shadow, brown eyeliner, and mascara so finely applied it was difficult to tell whether she was wearing false eyelashes. Her brows were beautifully shaped. *She's older than she looks*, Charlotte thought. *And she's definitely had a little work done around the eyes, and maybe the jawline.* But it was well done, subtle, and whoever had done it had known when to stop. The result took ten years off her.

"Well, we'll leave you to settle in," Charlotte said. "There's a house phone on the end table, and my number is right beside it. Just dial the four digits if you need me. I'm in the bungalow nearest the hotel. It's the first one we passed on the way here. Oh, and we've got in a few groceries for you . . . milk, butter, coffee, cheese, eggs, strawberries, bread . . . that sort of thing, so you can make yourself a light supper. Or, if you prefer, you can ring the hotel and they'll send something over."

Audrey's eyelids fluttered open. "Thank you. I'd like a bath and then a quiet evening and early night. I expect I'll be meeting the director tomorrow, and we can start discussing how he envisions my role."

"Oh, I'm sorry," said Charlotte. "I should have explained that to you. Our director, Simon Dyer, asked me to pass on his apologies. He wanted to be here to greet you and he would have been, but he had to leave suddenly for a family bereavement in Colorado. We're expecting him back within the next day or two. In the meantime, he's asked that we schedule costume fittings for you. And in case he's delayed longer, he's left notes for Aaron, our stage manager, so we can get a rehearsal or two under way."

Audrey shifted her position so she could see her sister. The corners of Maxine's mouth sagged into a formidable scowl, but she said nothing.

"It's a bereavement, Maxine. He had no choice. He had to go. We'll just have to make the best of it."

"Exactly," said Charlotte. "Well, we'll leave you to it. And as I said, call me if you need anything."

*

Charlotte and Paula Van Dusen strolled the short distance to Charlotte's bungalow. "Drink?" Charlotte asked.

"I don't know about you, but I need one."

Although Charlotte had known about the influential and wealthy Van Dusen family for years, and Paula had been involved with the board of directors and fundraising activities of the theater, the two women had got to know each other just a few months earlier when a body had been found in the garden of Oakland, following the theater company's outdoor performance of *A Midsummer Night's Dream*.

With a new British star joining the company, Paula had offered to take on the refurbishing of the bungalow. She'd been on site almost every day, giving orders and checking that deliveries arrived on time, and during the course of the project, she and Charlotte became friends. Paula was lonely, and in Charlotte she had found someone who didn't want or need anything from her. Not her name to lend to a cause, not her time, and above all, not her money. Charlotte had no agenda and wasn't interested in what Paula could do for her. Paula had found that hugely refreshing and had been drawn to Charlotte for her honesty, sophistication, sense of humor, and common sense.

While Paula fetched a bottle of gin from the drinks table in Charlotte's sitting room, Charlotte placed two highball glasses on the counter, opened the fridge, and pulled out a can of tonic. She stepped aside while Paula added a few ice cubes from the door dispenser to the glasses and assembled the drinks.

"I don't suppose you've got any limes?" Paula asked. "For a wedge to add to the drinks."

"Sorry, no. But I'll get some in for next time. There's a lemon, though. Will that do?"

"Certainly." When she'd added a lemon wedge to each drink, Paula asked, "Where would you like to sit?"

"How about outside? It's such a lovely afternoon."

When they were settled in Adirondack chairs positioned at the front of the bungalow to overlook the river, Charlotte asked Paula what she thought of Audrey.

"She seemed nice enough, but it's hard to tell. I would imagine there's a lot of stress involved in starting a new job where you don't know anybody. She's joining a company that's already jelled. And then there was the disappointment of the director not being here to meet her, and she's just got in from a long flight."

"Speaking of the flight, it was awfully good of you to send Barnes to meet them at the airport. I'm sure Maxine thought driving from JFK to the Catskills in a vintage Roller is exactly the way Audrey should be treated."

Paula smiled. "Well, I thought it would get things off to a good start. Her joining our little company was all very last minute, and it was fortunate, I thought, that she was available and agreed to come here." She paused for a moment to consider what she'd just said. "I'm sorry, maybe that didn't come out right. I didn't mean . . ."

Charlotte laughed good-naturedly. "I know what you meant, and I thought the same thing. She's been a big star in the UK since she was a child—what on earth does she want with a small Shakespeare theater company affiliated with a Catskills hotel in upstate New York? She'd play Broadway in a heartbeat, of course, but the likes of us here in Walkers Ridge? Still, we might seem like a small, underfunded company, but we are professional and we've got a solid reputation. We're proud of the work we do. We manage to create a little more magic with a lot less budget than most companies have to work with."

She paused for a moment, then continued. "And many young actors who are serious about getting into traditional theater want to start their careers with us for the training and discipline. We get far more applications than we have room for.

"As for Audrey, we'll find out in due course what really brought her here. In my experience, most of the older actors are either running away from something or have nothing left to lose. But there's a third group, and these are the ones who bring joy. For them, the opportunities may have dried up, but they still want to perform. They want to continue to practice their craft in front of an audience, and they aren't bothered by how much it pays, how big the audience is, or how grand the theater."

"There're some curtains in the barn. Let's put on a show!" said Paula.

"Exactly. But the thing is, they're all in it for something. So we'll see what brings Audrey here. She'll have a good reason." Charlotte took a sip and smacked her lips with a satisfied *Ah* as the crisp lemony drink caught the back of her throat and infused her senses. "I wonder why gin is considered a summery drink when it tastes the way a Christmas tree smells," she remarked.

"No idea," said Paula as she drained the last of her drink and stood up. "To me it tastes all-year-round-ish. I'm going to fix myself another one. How about you? Are you ready for another?"

Charlotte shook her head. "No, just the one for me, thanks."

"I'll just have a small one, and then I'd better see what Barnes is up to. It's been a long day for him, at his age. Normally, he hates turnpike driving. He just likes meandering along our little two-lane blacktop highways, but he seemed quite keen at the prospect of picking up Audrey from the airport."

With a small sigh, Paula disappeared around the side of the bungalow and through the door that opened into the kitchen.

Charlotte leaned back in her chair and closed her eyes. Normally careful about sun exposure, she was enjoying the sensation of the late afternoon sun warming her face when her phone rang. She answered and listened for a few seconds, then, her body stiffening, she straightened up in her chair and asked a series of pointed questions. As she ended the call, Paula returned and slid into the chair beside her.

"We've got a problem," Charlotte said. "A big one. I'll have that drink after all."

Chapter 2

"He can't bail on us just like that! Can he?" Paula demanded. "What does his contract stipulate?"

"I don't know. Harvey will have a copy of it somewhere in that messy office of his, along with all the other contracts. Simon told me he'd just spoken with Harvey and was letting me know 'as a courtesy.' A courtesy! We were planning to start a theater school together to accommodate all those students who can't get into New York schools, and now it looks as if that's down the pan. All that research and planning for nothing." She got to her feet, brushed her dark hair off her forehead, and scowled.

"What about the legalities of your theater school?" Paula Van Dusen asked.

"Money from investors will need to be returned. Fortunately we hadn't bought a property yet, so the legal affairs could have been much more complicated than they are. Simon said he'll send something in writing to make it all official. Of course he apologized and said he felt very bad, letting us all down like this. Which he certainly did. His leaving at this time is very hard on the cast. They've got to learn to work with a new lead actress—and now a new director as well." She sat down and met Paula's eyes. "He said he'd left behind a few staging notes for *Much Ado*, as well as the rehearsal notes he left with Aaron."

"Did he say why he's not coming back? I hope he had a very good reason."

"Well, his father's just died and his mother isn't doing very well, and he said he doesn't feel comfortable leaving her."

"I must say, I find this very inconvenient. But I think from now on, the board—and by that, I suppose I mean me—should retain copies of all theater contracts or at least duplicates. Well, we'll just have to find ourselves another director. And fast."

"We will. But it shouldn't be too hard to find somebody. There'll be someone hanging about off Broadway, perhaps, dying for a nice opportunity like this."

Paula heaved a deep sigh and took a sip of her refreshed drink.

"I don't want to make it sound too easy, though," said Charlotte. "We do have to be a bit choosy and make sure we get the right person. We need someone who understands the demands of staging Shakespeare. And Audrey has director approval, so whoever we bring in, she has to approve him."

"Is that likely to be a problem?"

"It shouldn't be. It hasn't been in the past with any other star actor. They were just happy to be offered the work and signed their contracts with the director who was already in place. The difference here is that Simon offered her the part, and she signed a contract agreeing to work with him. Now that Simon's out and a new director's coming in, she gets to approve him. Still, I don't see that being a problem because I doubt she even knows any American directors—what could she possibly object to?"

Charlotte checked her watch. "Let's see now. With Audrey and Maxine just arrived today and settling in, it's too late to mention this to them now, but we'll have to let them know tomorrow morning. I'll make a few calls to see who's available, and at least that way we might be able to suggest a few directors when we tell them."

"Does anyone spring to mind?" Paula asked.

"I know one or two, but whether they're free or not I won't know until I speak to them."

"Actually, I might know someone," said Paula. "Wade Radcliffe. He's local, and you might remember he was being considered when Simon was appointed. Wade was crushed when we chose Simon over him, and he might be very glad to have another chance at this job. I'll give him a call and see if he's interested. He might have retired, for all I know." She drained her glass. "Thank you for the delicious drinks. Really hit the spot. But now, I must be off."

"And I'd better get inside and start making phone calls. Ray'll be home soon, and I have no idea what we'll do for dinner."

"Oh, that reminds me," said Paula. "I intend to give a little dinner party when Audrey's a bit more settled. You and Ray, of course; Harvey and his wife; Audrey; Maxine; and any board members who can make it are welcome, and I was going to ask Simon, but now it'll be the new director, whoever he is. What do you think?"

"Lovely idea. You give the nicest dinner parties. Everyone will look forward to it."

"Well, call me tomorrow. I'll have to notify the board about this development and call a meeting, if anyone's available. Everybody travels so much these days. Never mind. We'll deal with it. We always do. Our theater company's come through much worse than this, believe me."

She handed Charlotte her empty glass and set off.

*

Charlotte was flipping through her Rolodex at the kitchen table when the door opened and a uniformed police officer entered. She looked up and smiled as he approached her and took her in his arms.

"Good day?" Ray Nicholson asked. "Did your actress arrive as planned?"

"She did," Charlotte replied as he released her. "That was the good news. The bad news is that Simon bloody Dyer has quit."

"Oh, no," said Ray. "You can't put on plays without a director."

"No, you can't. At least you can't mount a new play without a director. The director's all about getting the play ready for opening night, and then once all the decisions are made and it's up and running, other people, like the stage manager, pretty much take it from there. But we've got a new actress and she's going to need rehearsals, so we need to bring in a new director who can work with her and just generally manage the fall season." She indicated the Rolodex and notebook. "That's what all this is about. I'm beating the bushes to see who's available, and Paula thinks she might know someone, so between us, hopefully we can find someone quickly to step in and fill Simon's shoes."

Ray opened the fridge and pulled out a beer. Charlotte took this as a signal that his workday as chief of police of Walkers Ridge was over. If he had any reason to think he could get called back to work tonight, he'd have opted for a soda.

He tipped his head back as he drank out of the bottle and then set it on the table.

"Have you had a chance to think about what this means for us?"

"No, I . . ." Her voice trailed off as she realized what he meant. She and Ray were planning a trip in late October to visit Charlotte's mother in England, and while there, they intended to get formally engaged.

"Well, let's see what happens," said Ray. "You might get everything sorted out quickly and our plans won't be affected at all. But if need be, we'll just have to think of something else. Maybe we could go for the holidays instead."

"Yes," agreed Charlotte. "That could work. Mum would love us to spend Christmas with her."

Leaving his beer on the table, Ray disappeared into the bedroom. He returned a few minutes later, having swapped his uniform for a pair of comfortable beige cargo shorts and a dark-green golf shirt. He picked up his beer. "Why do you have to get involved in choosing the new director?" he asked, tipping the bottle toward her to emphasize the word "you." "I wouldn't have thought that would be part of your job description."

"In a larger company, it wouldn't be. Hiring a new stage director would fall to the artistic director, but we're such a small company, we don't have an artistic director, per se. In our case, the board chooses the director, who then takes on the roles of both artistic director and stage director. He chooses the plays and casts and directs them. But there are advantages for me in helping choose the director—hopefully the person who gets hired is someone I want to work with. I didn't have much input, though, when Simon was chosen."

Rupert, asleep in his basket, stirred. Charlotte glanced at him and then continued.

"The thing is, we need to get a replacement director ASAP. Since it was announced that Audrey Ashley would be joining us for the fall season, we've practically sold out. The PBS crowd is coming to see her because she was in that period drama everybody loved so much, and if we can turn those audience members into subscribers for next season, so much the better. We don't want to have to cancel performances and refund money. We don't want the theater dark. That would mean people cancel their hotel bookings, the restaurants in town lose money, and so on. The theater is the main attraction in Walkers Ridge, and we take that responsibility seriously. We do a lot for the local economy."

The theater operation dated back to the 1950s, when Harvey Jacobs's grandmother came up with the idea that a summer Shakespeare festival would be the perfect cultural attraction to lure guests to Jacobs Grand Hotel. Back then, the Catskills were flourishing as a holiday destination for New Yorkers, but within two decades, the great days of the hotels and resorts ended, and most of the buildings were abandoned or lost to fire. But with help from its annual Shakespeare festival, Jacobs Grand Hotel kept going, year after lean year. And now that upstate New York was experiencing an economic resurgence thanks to upwardly mobile New Yorkers flocking to the area in search of craft beers, artisan baking, and fine dining featuring fresh, local produce, the area was once again thriving. And so was Jacobs Grand Hotel. Rooms were being refurbished and modernized, more staff were being hired, and autumn bookings were better than they'd been in years.

Charlotte, who had begun her career as a costume designer with the venerable Royal Shakespeare Company in Stratford-upon-Avon, had found her way to the Catskills ten years ago after working on a Broadway production. Having grown up in an English village, small-town life in Walkers Ridge suited her, and she enjoyed working for the small theater company. She also worked on a freelance basis on Broadway productions and, through that work, had made connections that might be about to come in handy.

"I shouldn't have had the beer," Ray remarked, touching his stomach and offering a slightly sheepish grimace. "I would have been better going to the gym."

"How about a walk before dinner? You can take Rupert while I finish going through these cards, and when you get back, we'll cook dinner together."

"Good idea."

Chapter 3

In the gray light before dawn, Rupert stood by the bed, watching and waiting. His patience was rewarded when Ray slid his legs over the side of the bed. A moment later when the bathroom door clicked shut, signaling Ray was getting ready to report for the early shift, Rupert launched himself on the bed and hunkered down beside Charlotte. She put an arm around him, pulled him close to her, and the two drifted lazily in and out of sleep for another hour. When they awoke, the morning light was beckoning through the curtains, spilling warm little puddles of sunshine on the floor. Rupert stirred beside her, and together they welcomed a new day.

A few minutes later, they set off on their inspection of the peaceful morning-hushed grounds of Jacobs Grand Hotel, where Rupert could safely explore off leash. He took off eagerly down the path, rushing past the neighboring director's bungalow. *I hope nobody expects me to pack up and ship Simon's things*, thought Charlotte as she trotted along behind Rupert. *And what about returning the key? Simon's got some logistics to sort out with Harvey's office.* She and Rupert walked on until they reached the property line, then turned and began to retrace their steps toward home, walking a little slower on the return journey, both looking forward to their breakfast.

When they reached the director's bungalow, Charlotte hesitated and then, calling Rupert to her, turned up the short path that led to the entrance.

She climbed the three steps and tried the door. To her surprise, and then dawning realization, it was unlocked. She stepped into the kitchen but, without glancing around and with Rupert at her side, moved straight on to the sitting room, through the heavy stillness of space that had been unoccupied for a time, and into the bedroom.

The blue-and-white-striped curtains were closed, but in the muted light that filtered through, she could make out that the matching bedspread had been loosely pulled up. She flicked on the overhead light. She gazed around the room and saw no personal effects. Not a photo in a frame, a book on the bedside table, or a box of tissues. She checked the closet. Empty. She grasped the metal pull on the top drawer of the bureau and opened it, but she knew from the lightness of it as it slid toward her what she would see when it was open: nothing.

A mounting sense of confused disbelief mixed with betrayal flooded her. It was one thing to return home for a few days upon the death of a parent, but there had to be more to his not returning than his reluctance to leave his mother or he would have assumed he was coming back and would not have taken all his belongings with him.

Simon had known when he left for Colorado that he was leaving for good and had done the cowardly thing and just packed up and left without telling her. They'd collaborated over the past year on successful theatrical productions and had laid the foundation of what could have been a successful theater school. What was he up to? And why would he feel he had to do a runner?

She took note of the kitchen more closely as she and Rupert passed through on their way out. Like the rest of the bungalow, it was clean and neat. Dishes had been washed and put away and the counter cleared except for one thing: a key. Just the key, with no note. As a rush of anger surged through her veins, she locked the door to the bungalow, pocketed the key, and walked with Rupert back to the path that led to her bungalow and then on to the hotel.

Just as they reached the path, the door to the neighboring star bungalow opened and Audrey emerged, looking trim in a pair of black slacks and a long-sleeved white pullover with a brightly patterned turquoise scarf draped around her neck. She waved at Charlotte and walked purposefully along the path toward her.

Her makeup had been applied with a light, skillful touch, and in the soft early morning light, she looked fresh and youthful. "Good morning," Charlotte greeted her. "I hope you slept well."

"Oh, yes, I did, thanks, but I can't say the same for Maxine. The bed was heavenly. I was asleep almost as soon as you left. I've been up for a couple of hours already, catching up with the British news. Honestly, I don't know how we traveled before the days of Wi-Fi."

"I don't know how we did anything."

Audrey smiled and motioned to the hotel. "I'm not really one for a big breakfast. No full English for me, thanks. A bit of fruit is all I usually have, and sometimes a piece of toast with marmalade. I wondered if the hotel might do such a thing."

"Of course they can do that for you. If you can give me a few minutes to feed Rupert and get changed, I'd be happy to walk over with you, and then after breakfast, I can give you a little backstage tour."

"Oh, that sounds good. Shall we meet up, in say twenty—no, better make it thirty minutes? That should give you plenty of time. I'll see how Maxine is doing and if she's ready to join us. She's been up since all hours working on e-mails."

"Perfect. I'll see you in about half an hour."

*

Charlotte set out Rupert's breakfast and then headed for the shower. When she returned ten minutes later to check on him, he was in his basket, following her movements through adoring, contented brown eyes.

"Good boy," she said in that slightly higher-pitched voice dog owners use to speak to their beloved pets. "I'm just going to get dressed." She disappeared again, and Rupert closed his eyes. He opened them a little when the phone on the table jingled a tinny little tune, but it soon stopped and he went to sleep.

Dressed for the day, Charlotte returned to the kitchen and gathered up her tote bag and phone. One missed call: Paula. She pressed the return call button, and a moment later, Paula was letting her know she'd been in touch with Wade Radcliffe, who was very much available and keen to help in any way he could, and could Audrey be available for a meeting this morning at eleven o'clock?

"I'm just off to have breakfast with her now," Charlotte said. "I'll get back to you as soon as I can, but tell Wade we'll see him at eleven. We can all meet up in my office and go together to the read-through room."

After saying good-bye to Rupert, she found Audrey and Maxine waiting for her on the path to the hotel. They made polite small talk as they walked, with Charlotte briefly answering Audrey's question on how she'd ended up in the Catskills.

"I'm sure there's a wonderful story there," Audrey said. "I did hear you had previously been with the RSC. We must have just missed each other."

They had reached the back door of the hotel and Charlotte pulled it open. "The cafeteria is along here to the right," she said. "This is for theater people and hotel staff. We don't eat in the main dining room with the guests."

Maxine's eyebrows shot up as they entered the cafeteria and she took in the plastic tables and chairs. "Here?" she asked. "Audrey's expected to take her meals here?" Charlotte nodded as she placed a tray on the rail that ran along in front of the service area, where trays of scrambled eggs, sausages, and bacon were set over pans of simmering water. A help-yourself display featured small bowls filled with fresh fruit and individual servings of cereal and small containers of yogurt.

"You can take what you like from here," said Charlotte, gesturing to the fruit and yogurt, "but if you want something cooked for you, just tell them what you'd like and they'll prepare it for you. As for payment, once you're properly set up, you'll be given an account number for the cafeteria and everything is charged to that, as part of the room and board clause in your contract. But for today, we'll put everything on my account."

"Yes, I see. Well, let's have a go." Audrey slid the tray along, and when she reached the server, she ordered, "One slice of brown toast, with marmalade, and a pot of tea, please." Using a pair of tongs, the server placed a piece of toast on a bread-and-butter plate and handed it to Audrey. She then shifted her attention to Charlotte. "What can I get you?"

"I'm just having a coffee, thanks," she said.

"I'll just have a coffee too," said Maxine. "I had breakfast earlier at the bungalow."

Audrey hesitated over the yogurt, selected a serving of fruit, and when they arrived at the checkout, the cashier placed three empty mugs on their tray, and Charlotte gave her an account number.

They moved on to an assortment of condiments and utensils on a small bistro-style table. Charlotte pulled a knife and spoon from the cutlery baskets, and Audrey scanned the selection of jams and jellies, butter and margarine, all prepackaged in individual packets, and placed a couple on the tray. Charlotte and Maxine filled their mugs from the coffee dispenser machine, and Charlotte added a splash of cream to hers. Seeing Audrey hesitate, she showed her how to unwrap her tea bag, place it in the mug, and cover it with hot water from a giant silver-colored urn. They then made their way to a clean, empty table, and Charlotte lifted the items off the tray.

"There you go," she said, setting Audrey's fruit, tea, and toast in front of her.

Audrey eyed her mug of tea. "I'm sorry, but I couldn't possibly drink that."

"I know what you mean, but it's the way it's done in the cafeteria. There are no teapots. Maybe you'll get used to it. Or next time, you could bring your teapot and cup with you. Nobody would mind. In the meantime, would you like me to get you some coffee instead?"

"No, thank you. I'll just have the toast." Under Maxine's watchful, sympathetic eye, she hacked the slice of toast in half, peeled back the top of the butter packet, spread a bit on the piece of toast, added a dollop of marmalade from another packet, and nibbled at the corner.

"Now then," said Maxine, leaning on the table and wrapping her hands around her coffee mug, "why don't you tell us what Audrey is expected to do today."

"We've scheduled a meeting for her with the director at eleven."

"Oh, he's back then, is he?"

"Well, no, not exactly. We learned last night that, unfortunately, Simon Dyer won't be coming back. He's decided to stay out in Colorado. It's a terrible inconvenience to everyone, so we're asking another director—who is local, known to the theater, and can be ready to go quickly—to step in. His name is Wade Radcliffe, and he's the one you'll be meeting this morning."

With a little moue of disgust, Audrey replaced the piece of toast on the plate. Charlotte wasn't sure if she was reacting to the news about the director or if the marmalade hadn't quite met her English expectations.

"Audrey is contracted to work with Simon Dyer, not some other fellow we don't know," said Maxine. "We researched Mr. Dyer's credentials thoroughly before agreeing to work with him, so we will have to discuss this new development, and, of course, I'll have to review the contractual obligations."

"By all means, have a chat," said Charlotte, "but in the meantime, it would be helpful if you'd just agree to attend the meeting at eleven. We're so short on time to get this production up and running, and we do need everyone's cooperation."

"Of course I'll be there." Audrey smiled graciously.

"Thank you," said Charlotte. "We appreciate that." She looked from one to the other. "I guess we'll leave it there for the moment. Now, Audrey, on the way over here, you asked me how I landed in the Catskills, and I'm curious to know the same about you. What made you agree to come out here?"

"Oh," said Audrey, poking at an orange segment with her fork. "I had the time. I've been signed for a starring role as Queen Victoria in a BBC production, but it doesn't start filming until late winter, so I had the time for another project and thought this one might be fun." She leaned forward and said in a lower voice, "And I heard on the grapevine that a rather special honor might be coming my way in the New Year."

Picking up on the slight emphasis on the words "New Year," Charlotte leaned forward, mirroring Audrey's body language, and gave her a conspiratorial smile.

"Oh, and what might that be, I wonder?"

"Oh, come now, Charlotte! You've been around long enough to know one doesn't want to jinx one's chances by speaking too soon. For example, it's much better to let others suggest how perfect you'd be in a role and then humbly protest." She cast her eyes around the almost empty cafeteria. "But since you ask, and I know it will go no further, I have it on good authority that I'm going to be made a dame of the British Empire in the New Year's Honours list. But one is simply not permitted to breathe a word of it. I will be notified in early December, and then I have to keep it absolutely to myself until the official announcement on New Year's Day. So it's critically important that this role here in America goes well and generates lots of good press for the British papers to pick up. The *New York Times* and national television programs, I hope. You understand how important media are to one's career. I hope to meet soon with the theater's media relations person so we can get press kits organized and set up interviews and so on."

"Audrey, I'm not sure how this theater company was represented to you, but I'm afraid we don't really have a media relations person. But I'd be happy to introduce you to our local arts reporter, and I'm sure he'd be interested in doing a story."

"It's not ideal, but we could start with that, I suppose, although it's a bit early." Her lips formed a little pouty frown that Charlotte thought had been used many times to get her what she wanted.

Maxine having finished her coffee, and aware that Audrey was unlikely to eat or drink anything, Charlotte asked, "Well, what would you like to do now? Would you like a backstage tour?"

Audrey consulted her watch and glanced at Maxine. "I think I'll go back to my bungalow and brew myself a proper cup of tea, in a pot, and then I'll be back in time for the meeting with the director, and you can show me around if you think you must. I don't imagine there's all that much to see. I am familiar with theater dressing rooms, and in my experience, most backstage areas are pretty much the same. I can find my way around them perfectly well."

"Of course you can. Well, I'll be working in my office in the costume department this morning, so perhaps you can find your way there, and I'll help you get orientated on the way to the meeting. Paula Van Dusen will meet us in my office so we can all go together."

Chapter 4

Paula Van Dusen arrived just a few minutes before eleven, escorted by a tall, lean man with thinning gray hair who appeared to be in his early sixties. His rimless eyeglasses gave him a studious, stern look that contrasted with his blue jeans and white shirt. As Paula introduced Wade Radcliffe to Charlotte, he offered her an earnest smile. They shook hands, but before Charlotte could invite them to sit down, Audrey appeared in the doorway. Freshly styled blonde curls framed her perfectly made-up face. She entered the room with a graceful stride and smiled at everyone. Maxine sloped in after her, clutching her battered leather briefcase in both arms.

"We're not late, I hope," Maxine said. "As you can imagine, I've been frantically busy with e-mails and phone calls."

"I saw you perform in England," Wade said to Audrey when Paula introduced them. "You were absolutely marvelous."

Introductions complete, the five set off for the room down the hall used for script read-throughs.

Most of the space was taken up by a boardroom table that could comfortably seat twenty, but five drinking glasses and a pitcher of water at one end indicated where they should sit. They took their places and Paula opened the conversation.

"Well, Miss Ashley—"

"Oh, please, call me Audrey."

"Audrey. And Maxine. Thank you for agreeing to meet with Wade on such short notice, and we apologize that our previous director has seen fit—that is, won't be returning to us. However, we do need to get our fall season under way as smoothly as possible, and Wade has a lot of experience with large- and small-scale productions and has done Shakespeare many times, so he can do this for us, and we were delighted that he was available."

Wade acknowledged her remarks with a light smile and a small tip of his head.

Audrey nodded every now and then to show she was listening to the director as he described his vision for the production of *Much Ado About Nothing* in general and Audrey's role as Beatrice in particular. Charlotte made costuming notes as he laid out his concept for a production with a traditional Elizabethan look. Maxine remained silent but also took a few notes.

He carefully skirted the issue of Audrey's age, using soft, flattering words intended to ingratiate himself with her. Audrey signaled she'd heard enough by sitting back in her chair, folding her hands in her lap, and turning expectantly to Maxine, who shook her head lightly.

"Well, Wade, unless you have any questions, or anything to add, I think that wraps everything up," said Paula.

"I just want to say how much I'd love to work with Miss Ashley, and I'd be thrilled to take on this project."

"Wonderful, Wade," said Paula. "Thank you so much for coming in. We'll just have a little chat amongst ourselves, and I'll be in touch soon." The four women remained seated as Wade showed himself out.

"Well, I thought that went well," said Paula to Maxine. She turned to Audrey. "What did you think?"

"I'm sure he's a brilliant director," she said, "and whilst I was most impressed by his experience, unfortunately, I don't think he's quite right for me." Charlotte groaned inwardly.

Maxine set her briefcase on the desk, unzipped it, and folded it open. After removing a purple file folder, she zipped the briefcase back up and set it on the floor beside her chair. Opening the file folder, she removed a stack of a dozen or so pages. "As I'm sure you're aware," she said with a pointed nod in Paula's direction, "Audrey's contract"— she placed her hand on the papers for emphasis—"gives her director approval. If she chooses not to work with the new director you have chosen, that is her right."

"But . . ." Paula started to protest.

"However, we do have a director in mind who would be perfect," Maxine said smoothly. Paula tipped her head to one side as Maxine continued. "Yes, I've been speaking to someone in London this morning, and subject to a few conditions, he's willing to come out and take over the project. And he's the director Audrey wants to work with." She slid a piece of paper across the desk to Paula. "Here's his information and his agent's details. You can send the paperwork to the agent."

"Audrey," said Charlotte, "might I just ask why you want this particular director? Have you worked with him before?"

"Oh, yes. Edmund directed me in a play last year in Manchester. *Serious Charges*, it was called. Hugely successful run. We just worked so well together, and we always said we'd love to work together again, given the chance. I know he'll help me bring something special to this role that no one else could. I trust him. And this could be the perfect opportunity for him to get his name known in American theatrical circles. From here to Broadway! Who knows?"

She gave a delicate little shrug, accompanied by a coy smile that said more than she probably intended.

"And as he won't arrive for several days at least, I thought I'd spend some time in New York City. There doesn't seem to be much to do around here. Could the Rolls-Royce be ready at, say, two o'clock to drive us into Manhattan?" She stood up. "Thank you so much. You've been very kind."

Signaling that the discussion was over, Maxine gathered up her papers. When they had gone, Audrey leaving a light trail of an expensive fragrance in her wake, Paula turned to Charlotte and let out an exasperated sigh.

"Can you see the steam coming out my ears?" she demanded. "The Rolls-Royce indeed. Barnes can drive them to Rhinecliff and they can take the Amtrak from there. They're lucky we're not putting them on the Trailways bus."

"They knew all along they weren't going to have Wade," mused Charlotte. "They sat through that whole interview pretending to be interested, letting the poor man talk, when they came prepared to request their own director."

"Wade's going to be devastated," said Paula. "Twice he's been up for our directing job, and twice he wasn't chosen. It will be really hard on him. I wonder if there's anything else we can do." Her fingers played with the pearls at her throat. "What about this? We apologize, explain the situation so he knows it wasn't our choice, and we offer him a smaller job with the company."

"You can try," said Charlotte, "but he seemed like a proud man, and I don't think he'd settle for someone else's table scraps." Paula winced. "In fact," Charlotte continued, "he might see that as an insult. And what about the budget? We don't have enough money, surely, to create an extra position just for him. But I do agree he's going to be very disappointed. And more than a little angry, would be my guess."

"Actually," said Paula, "before this goes any further, I need to get my hands on a copy of her contract. I want to check out the director approval business for myself."

"Good idea. But to bring in a director from the UK to work here on such short notice—won't there be an issue getting him a work visa or whatever it's called?" asked Charlotte. "It's been ten years since I went through the process, and anyway, the RSC sorted it all out for the company. Surely getting him the documentation he needs will take months—much longer than we've got. Every day that this production isn't in preparation is time wasted and could end up costing us money if we aren't ready to open on time."

"It shouldn't be a problem," said Paula. "Nancy'll take care of the paperwork, and it can be issued through the US Embassy in London in three to five working days, although even that's a delay we don't need. This director those two want could be on his way by the end of next week. That is, if he even agrees to come here at the salary we're offering. I hope he won't. This really is going to make things difficult with Wade. He was desperate for this job, and I'm afraid I rather let him think he was a shoo-in for it."

Charlotte took a sip of water. "What's his name, this director Audrey wants?"

Paula glanced at the name on the piece of paper Maxine had handed her. "Edmund Albright."

Chapter 5

"Well here we go again," said Paula Van Dusen the following Friday. "Another arrival." For this one, however, there had been no refurbishment of the director's bungalow, no Rolls-Royce pickup at the airport, and no welcoming party on the front steps of the hotel.

Paula described the arrival plans as "a little more low-key." Charlotte dubbed them "a bit more down-market."

"I suppose just to be marginally polite, though, someone will have to say hello and hand over his key," said Paula.

"I can take care of that," Charlotte replied. "You've probably got better things to do."

"Not sure about better things to do, but I'm happy to let you handle it. I'm going to give this one a miss."

When the local taxi dropped off its passenger at the front door of the hotel, Charlotte stepped forward and, with what she hoped looked like a sincere smile, held out her hand as she introduced herself, adding, "And you must be Edmund Albright."

In his early thirties and wreathed in a self-satisfied air of youthful confidence, he gave her a practiced, charming grin as he brushed a floppy lock of brown hair off his forehead in a mannered, affected way. He wore a chocolate-brown cashmere sweater and carried a beige jacket draped over his arm. "Yes," he said with the faintest trace of a lisp, "that's me."

Charlotte welcomed him on behalf of the theater company and hotel and added, "The director's bungalow is down this way, if you'd like to follow me?" She picked up the smaller of his bags and led the way to the bungalow. She unlocked the door, opened it, and handed the key to the new occupant. "Again, welcome. We hope you'll enjoy your tenure with our company. We're all looking forward to working with you. The cast is eager to get on with rehearsals."

"As am I. And the call has gone out for . . . what time?"

"Nine o'clock Monday morning. You'll have a couple of days to settle in, and the cast will be in the auditorium, all bright-eyed and bushy-tailed and keen to meet you and to hear your thoughts."

"Excellent," said Edmund. "I've had a terrific idea for this production and can't wait to share it with everybody." He gave her a charming grin. "They're going to love it."

*

Carrying cups of Monday morning coffee from the cafeteria, the cast and crew of the Catskills Shakespeare Theater Company, some with their hair still wet from the shower, trooped into the theater and found seats in the first four rows. In the center of the first row, an empty seat on each side of her, sat Audrey, her eyes shining with excitement. The other actors, chatting eagerly to one another, did not include her in their conversations. But one actress, seeing Audrey on her own, hesitated, then approached her.

Small and trim, Mattie Lane wore her long brown hair piled on top of her head, held in place with a bright-red toothed clip. Her features were fine and delicate, and she walked with a fluid, graceful ease.

"Good morning," she said to Audrey. "I'm Mattie Lane. I can't tell you how thrilled I am to be working with you. May I . . . ?" She smiled and gestured at one of the empty seats.

"Yes, do, by all means."

Aaron, in charge of the meeting, scurried across the floor in front of the stage, stopping to exchange a few words with Mattie and then taking a seat at the end of the front row beside Charlotte. When a lone figure emerged from the wings and took center stage, talk immediately died down, replaced by an air of nervous anticipation, and all eyes, including Charlotte's and Aaron's, turned toward Edmund Albright. He was neatly dressed in the same beige slacks he'd worn on his arrival and the beige jacket he'd been carrying.

He gazed at his audience for a moment, then crossed the stage and lightly and smoothly descended the small set of stairs at one side that brought him to the same level as the cast. In a few long, swift strides, he was standing in front of them.

After introducing himself, he launched into a discussion of the themes and structure of the play. At first, the cast listened attentively, especially when he discussed the treatment of women in the play, but as he drifted into a lecture on when the play was written and how it fits into Shakespeare's body of work, the audience began to fidget. And then he took his remarks in an unexpected direction that snapped everyone, especially Charlotte, back to attention.

"Some of you may have read that wonderful essay by the late Sir Alec Guinness on the concept of performing Shakespeare's plays outside their usual Elizabethan and Jacobean time frame. Shakespeare has been performed in everything from Edwardian costumes to modern dress. You may have heard about the controversial production of Richard III with Ian McKellen, in which the cast wore Nazi costumes." Sensing where this was going, a low conversational buzz rippled through the audience. Knowing he now had their full attention, Albright continued. "So I'm proposing that our production of *Much Ado About Nothing* be set just after the Civil War, when the surviving soldiers return home." Charlotte and Aaron, immediately realizing the huge complications for costuming, turned to each other. Aaron shook his head and mouthed a silent "No way"; Charlotte replied an equally silent "Impossible," accompanied by a small but emphatic shake of her head.

"Now I know some of you might be a bit shocked by this idea," Albright went on, "but it's got your attention, hasn't it? And it's going to get everybody's attention! And once you've had a chance to think it over and get used to the idea, if you're not in favor of it now, I'm sure you'll warm to it and finally embrace it."

Charlotte leaned forward and scanned the faces of the cast members along the row, trying to gauge just how warmly they were embracing the concept. Some looked upset, others looked puzzled, but Audrey Ashley's expression had gone from one of open admiring anticipation before the director started speaking to one of horror, and Charlotte knew why.

The idea of dressing a forty-five-year-old woman, playing a part meant for someone half her age, in a Scarlett O'Hara–type costume with frills and a picture hat was appalling. Audrey no doubt feared she would look ridiculous and that when the publicity photos were released, she'd be a laughingstock. Edmund must surely realize that. And yet here he was, the new director, at Audrey's request. Audrey's narrowed eyes and tightly pinched lips indicated her reaction to Albright's announcement had changed from horror to hard anger.

*

"Of course it's not going to happen," spluttered Charlotte as she and Aaron walked back to the costume office when the meeting was over. "We couldn't possibly design and create all those costumes in time. And what's more, we don't even begin to have the budget for something like that. And think of the waste. They'd never be used again."

"What if he suggests we rent the costumes?" Aaron asked.

"Out of the question," said Charlotte. "We could never afford it. And what's more, he never should have made that announcement without consulting me. Now he's going to look like an idiot when he has to retract all that Civil War rubbish and tell the cast we're going ahead with a standard, normal production."

She unlocked the door to her office and tossed her notebook on her desk.

"I wonder why he would want to do that," mused Aaron. "Everybody likes Shakespeare just the way it is. It's what they expect. It's what they come for."

"Oh, I don't know about that. Lots of productions set in different times have been popular enough, but as you say, the purists like Shakespeare done the old-fashioned way, and you could very well be right that this type of production won't suit our audiences. Do you know, I don't think we've ever attempted to stage anything quite as outlandish as that. Probably because we don't have the resources or funds to take on such risk. A flop would be financially catastrophic. We just can't afford to have people stay away."

Charlotte was prevented from saying any more by her ringing telephone. "Oh, hello," she said. "Yes, he spoke to the cast." She paused to listen. "It was, shall we say, interesting." Another pause. "That's a good idea. See you when you get here."

Aaron stopped leafing through the paperback copy of *Much Ado About Nothing* he'd picked up off Charlotte's desk. "When who gets here?"

"Paula Van Dusen's on her way through town and has decided to stop in. She hasn't met our Mr. Edmund Albright yet. She thought it might be a good idea if she popped in to say hello."

Aaron coughed lightly and nodded, then raised the book slightly. "Has Edmund Albright actually read this? I wonder why he wants to do it this way. I don't see how it would work with a Civil War setting."

"Oh, I'm sure he's read it. And he's probably given a lot of thought to how he wants to stage it. But you raise a really good point when you ask why he would want to do it that way."

*

"The Civil War?" Paula Van Dusen clasped her hands to her chest as she doubled up with laughter. "You're pulling my leg."

"I wish I were," said Charlotte. "But that's what he said. And you should have seen the thunderous look on Audrey Ashley's face. If looks could kill."

That sent Paula into gales of laughter. "Oh, I'll bet poor old Wade Radcliffe with his stodgy, traditional version of the play's looking pretty good to her right about now."

"Well, let's go meet Edmund." Charlotte picked up her handbag. As they strolled through the backstage corridor that would bring them to the cafeteria and then the rear entrance to the hotel, Paula asked, "North or South?"

"North or South what?"

"Did Edmund Albright say if the characters would be representing the North or South? Or both? I'm not that familiar with the play. If it's the South, will it be all 'fiddledeedee' and 'after all, tomorrow is another day'?"

"No, it won't," said Charlotte. "I doubt he'd change the script. At least I hope not."

They passed Charlotte's bungalow and continued on to the director's. As they got closer, a loud voice coming from inside brought them up short, and they crept closer, pausing to listen. The door was open and a woman's voice carried clearly.

"I arranged for you to come here so you could help me. I trusted you to make me look good, and this is how you repay me?" The speaker paused, indicating that someone else was speaking, but Paula and Charlotte couldn't hear the response. "No, I absolutely will not do it like this. Over my dead body." A moment later, Audrey Ashley stormed out of the house and, throwing Charlotte and Paula a look filled with determined vengeance, thundered past them and turned down the path that led to her bungalow.

"Let's give her a few minutes and then look in on her when we've finished here," said Charlotte as Paula knocked on the door of Edmund Albright's bungalow.

"Come!"

They entered the bungalow to find Edmund standing in the middle of the sitting room with his arms folded. This bungalow was dull, dated, and dowdy, as the star bungalow had been before Paula's renovation. Everything in the sitting room, from carpet to curtains, was a tired, dreary shade of brown. *It wouldn't take too long to get depressed in here*, thought Charlotte as a feeling of something bordering on pity for Simon Dyer, the previous occupant, flashed through her mind. Maybe he left because he just couldn't take one more day in the bungalow.

"Hello, again, Edmund," said Charlotte. "I'd like to introduce you to Paula Van Dusen, the chairperson of our theater board."

Paula, in a pale-pink sleeveless summer dress, stood out like a buoy in the middle of a brown ocean. The two shook hands, and Paula asked if they might sit down.

"Forgive me," said Edmund. "Should have offered. Please." Charlotte and Paula sat on a brown corduroy sofa that sagged beneath their weight. They hauled themselves forward a little to perch on the edge. Edmund pulled a chair out from the table and sat facing them. He crossed one leg over the other and leaned back slightly.

"I can't offer you anything to drink, I'm afraid," he said. "I have no idea where the shops are, and I haven't had time to get anything in."

"No, of course not," said Charlotte, "but that's not why we're here." She threw a glance at Paula. "I'll come right to the point. We need to discuss that announcement you made this morning to the cast and crew about performing *Much Ado About Nothing* against a Civil War backdrop. The financial implications are enormous for the company, you see, and by rights you should have discussed your concept with us before dropping that bombshell." She smiled nervously. "I don't know how well the idea will go down with the cast, but it certainly has me very concerned, I must say."

"Oh, I'm sorry to hear that. I thought you would have been well up for a challenge. I heard you were with the RSC, so I wouldn't have thought this would be anything you couldn't handle."

"The RSC has a sizeable costume department and is well equipped and staffed to handle anything and everything," said Charlotte, "given enough time. The thing is"—she raised her hands in a fluttery little gesture—"here, there's just me and my assistant Aaron, who has to spread himself pretty thin over several production areas, so you see, your idea would place unrealistic demands on us."

Paula Van Dusen made a little throat-clearing noise, and Edmund turned his blue eyes to her.

"And not only do we have Charlotte's concerns to consider," Paula said, "but to put it bluntly, we simply don't have the budget for such an ambitious enterprise. Not for costumes, or sets, or anything. So I'm afraid the board simply can't authorize it."

"Not to mention the time factor," Charlotte chimed in. "We're on a very tight timeline to get that production up on its legs, with a new leading actress and a new director."

"So you see, for all the reasons we've given you, a Civil War production is absolutely out of the question," Paula concluded. "But I must admit I'm a bit curious. Why or how did you come up with the idea of that concept?"

"Well, during my research, I read about an RSC production that was set in a country house just after the First World War. And it was hugely successful, I might add. *Much Ado* opens with soldiers coming home from a war, so I thought because this is America, why not the Civil War? And because this is New York State, I thought why not the North?"

"So it's the North, not the South?" Paula asked.

"That's right. And you were there when I told the cast about it," Edmund said, turning to Charlotte. "You saw their reaction. They were gobsmacked! Think what the media will make of it. And is there a theater anywhere that couldn't do with a bit more press?"

"I just don't see it working for us," said Charlotte. "Our theater is all about classic Shakespeare. Our audiences are used to seeing the plays performed a certain way, and that's what they come for. They like the traditional versions."

"I do hope you won't take this the wrong way," Edmund said with a tired smile that came nowhere near his eyes, "but since when does the costume designer tell the director what kind of production we're having?" He leaned forward, clasping his palms together, resting his elbows on his knees. "It's up to me, as the director, to orchestrate the mounting of the production. I'm responsible for the overall practical and creative interpretation of the script. I have final say on the whole process, from design and preproduction to staging and execution. So you'll just have to find a way to get those costumes made."

He turned to Paula. "This is about my vision, not your budget. So you'll just have to find the money." His voice had a hard, cold edge to it, but, thought Charlotte, was there also the slightest hint of nervous doubt? He adopted a more conciliatory tone as he added, "You look like a resourceful woman. I'm sure if you both dig a little deeper, you can find a way to get this done."

Charlotte pressed her hand over her mouth as Paula rose to her feet, saying, "Well, you've certainly given us something to think about." Ice formed on every word. Her face was flushed, and her eyes were hard and glittery. "Don't bother showing us out, Mr. Albright. We know the way."

On the path outside, Paula put a reassuring hand on Charlotte's shoulder. "He shouldn't have spoken to you like that."

"Never mind me," said Charlotte. "The way he spoke to you! Honestly, I couldn't believe what I was hearing. You responded to him perfectly."

"Do you think so? I was seeing red, and I just couldn't be in the same room with him."

"The thing is, I really wanted this to work," said Charlotte as they set off on the short path that led to her bungalow. "I probably came across as resistant and stuck in my ways. I didn't mean to. I just feel so overwhelmed by the demands of what he's got in mind. There's so much work involved, and you know how much it'll cost."

"And," said Paula, "as you rightly pointed out, we have to consider our audience. What do they want? How would something like this go down with them? But don't worry. We'll deal with it."

"Yes we will. But honestly, that man! If he was made out of chocolate, he'd eat himself, as my mother used to say." Charlotte drew in a slow, steadying breath. "Let's get a drink. I know we were going to talk to Audrey, but we're in no mood for that right now."

"I agree. My heart's still pounding, and my blood pressure must be sky-high. I can't tell you how angry I am with that arrogant man. He's going to be nothing but trouble."

"The thing is, if Edmund doesn't work out, that could really mess up the plans Ray and I have. We're hoping to visit my mother in the UK in October and get engaged while we're with her. If I can get the costumes sorted quickly, he and I can go, but if this drags on too long, we won't be able to get away. And it's been so long since I've seen my mum."

"We'll do everything we can to make sure that happens," said Paula.

When they had almost reached Charlotte's bunga-low, Aaron emerged from the hotel and crossed the grav-eled parking area carrying a presentation bouquet draped across one arm. The cellophane packaging crackled as he got closer, and a light breeze ruffled the tails of the broad bright-pink ribbon as he walked toward them. When he reached them, he stopped.

"Who are they for?" asked Paula, peering at the lavish display of roses, lilies, carnations, chrysanthemums, and daisies nestled on a bed of baby's breath and ferns.

"Miss Audrey Ashley."

"Of course they are. Who are they from, I wonder?"

"An admirer, no doubt," said Charlotte. "I expect she gets lots of them." She reached out to the bouquet and turned over the florist's business card stapled to the cello-phane and noted the name. "Very nice. This should cheer her up. Hmm, I wonder if they're from Edmund. Is there a card from the sender?"

"I don't know," said Aaron. "There might be one inside. Why would I look? I was just told to deliver them, so that's what I'm doing."

"Well, they're certainly extravagant. Someone wants to make a good impression. I can't remember the last time anyone sent me flowers like that," said Paula. "And I haven't bought flowers from a florist in years. Of course, with Ned in charge of my garden, there's no reason why I would. He's got the greenest thumb in the Catskills."

Ned, the Van Dusen's head gardener, was almost seventy, and after a lifetime toiling in the Van Dusen orchard and flower and vegetable gardens, he was held in high regard throughout the county. He propagated and grew beautiful plants and had won dozens of first-place rosettes from the New York State fall fair for his efforts.

"From A Floral Affair, no less," said Charlotte in a flat voice, reading the name of the town's best florist off the card.

"Are you all right?" Aaron asked, peering at her. "You look, I don't know, upset. Are you upset? Has something happened?"

"No, everything's fine. You carry on, and I'll catch up with you later."

With a last worried look, Aaron left on his delivery, and Charlotte opened the door to her bungalow.

"We can't let this crazy production go ahead. It's just not possible," Paula Van Dusen said when they were standing in the kitchen. "I'll need to speak to the board and see what our options are. The way I see it, someone will either have to bring him to his senses or find a way stop him."

Chapter 6

"Here you go." Charlotte handed Paula a gin and tonic. "Let's sit down and talk this through. See what we can come up with."

Rupert joined Charlotte on the sofa, and after taking a small sip of her drink, she said, "I think Edmund's contract is the best place to start. Harvey's office should have a copy of it. We can check the wording around the budget. Normally, the play's producers provide a budget, and the director agrees to stay within it when he signs the contract. If that's the case here, that might be enough to shut down his Civil War idea."

"It might. I have no idea what's in his contract, so as you say, that's the best place to start. The awful thing is, we've been doing these productions for decades and have never run into a problem like this, and the contracts haven't been reviewed or updated in heaven knows how long. We'll have to be more careful in future.

"So let's drink up, and we'll see if we can have a chat with Harvey. He's the one who stands to lose the most from all this. He doesn't take much interest in the theater operations, but he cares passionately about his hotel business, and if we're late getting this show into performance, he'll lose bookings, as you know," said Paula.

"That's true."

"And we've got to get it stopped sooner rather than later. We want to get back on track before word gets out that the director's got this ridiculous notion of mounting a Civil War–type Shakespeare. It's got to be the craziest thing I've ever heard."

"That's probably why it's never been done before, at least not to my knowledge," said Charlotte. "Right." She drained her glass and stood up. "Should we ring Harvey or just show up?"

"Normally, I'd say we should call first, but in this case, let's just go over there and take our chances."

"He'll drop whatever he's doing to talk to you," said Charlotte. "He's got all the time in the world for you."

"And so he should. The amount of money I've poured into his hotel over the years! I've just done up one of his bungalows! The least he can do is be available when I need to speak to him."

They entered the hotel through the front entrance, passed the empty registration desk, and walked down a short corridor to Harvey Jacobs's office. His longtime secretary, Nancy, was seated at her desk typing into an elderly computer. She looked up as they approached and removed her dark-framed glasses. Although they were attached to a cord looped around her neck, she held them in her hand as she greeted them. A tall, thin woman, with gray wavy hair that aged her and an unlined, smooth complexion that gave her a more youthful appearance, she was of indeterminate age, but Charlotte reckoned she must be in her midsixties. She'd spent her entire working life at the hotel, having started as secretary to Harvey Jacobs's father right out of high school. It had been a sad day for Harvey a year or so ago when he'd had to tell Nancy that, because of the downturn in business, he could no longer afford to keep her on. But with a highly successful summer season behind them, things were looking up, and Nancy was back on a part-time basis.

"Oh, Mrs. Van Dusen. Hello. And Charlotte." She ran a finger down a page of the day planner open on her desk. "We weren't expecting you, were we?"

"No, Nancy, you weren't. But I need to speak to Harvey. It's important. Is he in?"

"He's always in for you, Mrs. Van Dusen. Except when he isn't actually here, of course." She knocked on the door to Harvey's office and opened it.

"Mr. Jacobs, Mrs. Van Dusen is here to see you. She says it's important."

"Of course. Show her in."

Nancy stood to one side as Paula Van Dusen and Charlotte entered, then closed the door behind them. Charlotte had been in Harvey Jacobs's office only a handful of times and was always struck by how cluttered it was.

Dark-green hotel registers with the years stamped in gold on their spines were stacked on overflowing bankers' boxes. Beige file folders bursting with yellowed documents teetered on top of wooden file cabinets with brass fittings, and the doors of the glass-fronted cabinets strained to hold back the contents pushing against them. Harvey's desk was awash in papers, and three stackable baskets marked "Read," "Sign," and "Recycle" stood empty. Charlotte suspected this room had been Harvey and Nancy's battleground for the last two decades.

Harvey scurried around the side of his desk to remove a cafeteria tray from one of the visitors' chairs and gestured to them. After a quick glance around the room, and an internal struggle about whether she should say something about the state of his office, Paula Van Dusen leaned forward and said, "Harvey, we've got a problem with the new director."

"I'm sorry to hear that." He made a hearty you've-come-to-the-right-person kind of gesture accompanied by a reassuring smile. "How can I help?"

"You can help by firing Edmund Albright."

The smile faded and his arms dropped to his side. "I'm sorry, Mrs. Van Dusen, but I couldn't possibly do that. I didn't hire the man. The theater board did. I'm not responsible for the theater personnel. You know that."

"Does he have to know that? We're desperate to get rid of him."

"Surely you aren't suggesting we should . . . and anyway, why would you want to fire him? That seems a bit drastic. He's only just arrived. He's barely had time to unpack. Shouldn't you give him a chance to work things out, whatever the problems are? Or are there cast problems? Does the leading actress, what's her name, not like him? Is that it?"

"Audrey Ashley," said Charlotte.

"She did like him," said Paula, "and in fact, he's here at her request. We brought him on board because she has director approval and she asked for him. She's not the problem. The problem is, she doesn't like how he wants to stage the production and what it will mean for her. Charlotte will explain all that to you."

Charlotte outlined the director's plans to mount an expensive Civil War–themed production. "We just don't have the resources to meet his demands," she said. "Costumes, sets . . . we can't do it, and we'd be crazy to try."

"And we certainly don't have the budget for it," added Paula.

Harvey rested his hands on his ample stomach. "I see. And there's also the timing issue. As I see it, you're burning daylight with this production as it is."

"That's right," said Paula. "And this situation could affect you too, Harvey. The hotel business has just started to turn around, and you don't want to lose that momentum. We're heading into fall—tourists coming to enjoy the fall leaves who want to include a visit to the theater. Lots of out-of-towners who need a place to stay for a night or two.

So the play must open on time—even a week's delay could make a difference in terms of canceled hotel bookings. And the production's got to be good—we've got to give the theatergoers what they want."

Harvey's eyebrows shot up. "I'm not sure what you expect me to do, but I'll try to think of something." He let out a resigned sigh. "I'll speak to Nancy. She's good at solving problems."

"You do that," said Paula Van Dusen. "And you can start by asking her to bring us a copy of Edmund Albright's contract."

Harvey spoke directly into the old-fashioned intercom box on his desk to relay Paula Van Dusen's request to his secretary.

"Right you are, Mr. Jacobs," came the disembodied reply through the tinny speaker. Nancy clung to the outdated workplace etiquette of referring to her boss as Mr. Jacobs, and finally, he had given up asking her to call him Harvey.

"She should have it for you on your way out," he said. "If I think of anything, I'll be in touch."

Paula Van Dusen stood up, signaling the meeting was over. Harvey opened the door and stood to one side as the women filed out.

"Here you are, Mrs. Van Dusen," Nancy said, handing her a large white envelope. "Didn't even have time to file it."

When they were gone, Nancy strode into Harvey's office.

"Did you get all that?" he asked, flipping the switch on the office intercom to the off position. She nodded grimly. "Got any ideas?"

She shook her head. "I read his contract. They can't fire him just because they don't like his production ideas, crazy though they may be. He's agreed to deliver a production of *Much Ado About Nothing*, and the contract doesn't specify what kind of production."

"What about the budget?"

"Doesn't say anything about that either. In fact, I didn't see any grounds at all for the board to terminate the contract."

"Not much of a contract, is it?" grumbled Harvey. "Not if you can't get out of it."

Nancy folded her arms, lowered her head, and fixed her brown eyes on him over the top of her glasses.

"Mr. Jacobs, you know I've given my entire working life to Jacobs Grand, and no one understands the workings of this hotel better than I do. I hear things. People come to me with their problems. And no one, not even you, has been through more ups and downs here than I have. And I can tell you that Mrs. Van Dusen is right about one thing. If this play doesn't open on time, or if it's a flop, the hotel's financial recovery is in jeopardy. And what's more, our reputation could be at stake. We're known for the high quality of our theatrical productions, and if this one comes across as ridiculous, that could impact us. The hotel and theater are meant to operate separately, but the fortunes of both are connected. And the truth is, the hotel needs the theater more than the theater needs the hotel. They could go somewhere else. We can't."

Harvey rubbed his chin as he thought about what she had just said. While he had no doubt as to Nancy's loyalty to the hotel, he knew she must also be concerned for herself. The past year, when she'd been laid off, had been difficult. Her mother had died, and although her death was expected, there'd been the unwanted expense of a funeral. Nancy continued to live in the small two-story duplex she'd shared with her mother, but on her salary, repairing the peeling gray asphalt siding that let in the damp and the old wooden frames that were beginning to rot was out of the question. Harvey had suggested that she sell the house and take up his offer of a room in the hotel, but so far, she had declined.

She gestured at his desk and let out a long, mournful sigh. "Mr. Jacobs, I do wish you'd let me tidy up these files. They look just awful when somebody comes into your office, especially someone important like Mrs. Van Dusen. What she must think of us."

Meanwhile, Charlotte and Paula Van Dusen walked in silence through the hotel's back corridors until they reached Charlotte's office.

"Nancy's an interesting character," said Charlotte as she unlocked the door. "I suspect during that period last winter when she was laid off that she was working for Harvey anyway."

"Volunteering, you mean. Probably. I suspect that her loyalty is to the hotel, not Harvey."

"I agree," said Charlotte. "And that gray suit she wears. She's had that ever since I've been here. I must admit, even though we've had lots of professional dealings over the years, I don't really know her very well. She seems a really private kind of person who doesn't mix much with the rest of us. For example, I've never seen her eat lunch in the cafeteria."

"She always went home for lunch," said Paula, "to check on her mother. She took care of old Mrs. Hargreaves through a long, terrible illness, and I expect poor Nancy incurred a lot of debt when she finally had to place her mother in a nursing home. Harvey felt terrible when he had to lay her off, especially as it was right around the time her mother died. But the hotel was doing so badly, he really had no choice, and Nancy understood that. For Nancy's sake, I really hope now that things have finally turned around, the hotel will keep going in the right direction."

"I hope so too." Charlotte set her bag down on the worktable and gestured to her desk. "Why don't you look through the contract while I make us a cup of tea."

She returned a few minutes later carrying two cups on a small tray. As Charlotte handed her a cup, Paula reached the same conclusion about the contract as Nancy had—that she couldn't see any grounds to fire Edmund.

"Incompetence?" Charlotte asked.

"How can he be incompetent? He hasn't even started."

"I know. Clutching at straws. Does it say anything about board approval?"

"Approval of what kind of production he wants to do?"

"Yes."

Paula scanned the contract. "No, it doesn't mention that."

"So unless he changes his mind, the Civil War theme is a go."

"Looks that way. But I can tell you one thing: the next director's contract will definitely spell out what we want. This will never happen again."

The two sat lost in thought, taking occasional sips of tea, until Charlotte broke the silence.

"Ha! 'Against my will I am sent to bid you come in to dinner.'"

"What?"

"It's from *Much Ado About Nothing.*" She got up and—with a quick glance in both directions, up and down the corridor—quietly closed the door. "Look, we're not going to get anywhere arguing with Edmund Albright. He's dug his heels in, so we'll have to try a different, softer approach. A little friendly persuasion. I suggest we move up the date of the dinner party you were planning to give, and we'll use what you call dinner diplomacy—a good meal and civilized conversation—to encourage him to abandon that crazy Civil War idea. Without actually telling him we think it's a crazy idea. Your Oakland is the American equivalent of a British country house, and in its genteel atmosphere, I suspect he'll be more open to hearing what we have to say. And if board members can be there, so much the better."

Paula was instantly alert. She pulled a thick engagement book with an elastic band around it from her purse and flipped it open. "How does Friday the thirtieth sound?"

"Fine."

"I'll send Barnes to pick up Audrey, Maxine, and Albright. And Ray could drive you and Harvey and his wife."

"I'll have to check with Ray. I hope he's not working an evening shift, but if he is, perhaps he could switch with someone."

"Any menu thoughts? Since our special guests are English, they might like lamb. Or roast beef and Yorkshire pudding?"

"I've got a feeling Audrey eats very light. Maybe fish? She could have hers just plain grilled if she wishes, and the rest of us could have a sauce."

"That's a thought. Or we could have a choice of entrée. And soup as a starter. I'll get the invitations written, and you can hand deliver them" She checked her watch. "I'd better let Barnes know I'm ready to go home. I hear he's been spending a lot of time in your canteen lately."

"Yes, he was going on about how you can't get decent pie these days."

Paula laughed. "Maybe I'd better suggest he spend his waiting time walking in the grounds rather than eating pie."

"Shall I ring the cafeteria to see if he's there?" Paula nodded, and a few minutes later, Charlotte informed her that Barnes was on his way.

"Fine. I'll be off. See you soon."

Charlotte wrapped up a few things in her office and then headed home. As she stepped on the path that led to her bungalow, a figure hurtled toward her. A moment later, she recognized Mattie, the young actress who had sat beside Audrey at the cast meeting that morning. Mattie had joined the company after the previous ingenue had died, and Aaron designed a Juliet dress for her. Charlotte had wondered at the time if there was something more between them, but if there had been, it had mellowed into friendship—as far as she could tell, they were not romantically involved. Aaron was, however, fond of her. That much Charlotte did know.

Head down, her hair loose and falling out of the clip that had held it in place on top of her head earlier in the day, Mattie charged on. She did not look at Charlotte, who leapt aside as she rushed past. She let out a choking sob, and Charlotte realized only then she was crying.

"Mattie!" she called out after the girl. But Mattie didn't turn around and sprinted in the direction of the hotel.

Charlotte gazed after her for a moment and then hurried home to Rupert.

After receiving an enthusiastic greeting, she clipped on his lead and they walked through the grounds, keeping to the path until they reached the star bungalow. The curtains were open, and the elaborate bouquet Aaron had delivered could be glimpsed in a vase on the table in front of the window.

They really are beautiful, she thought as she and Rupert continued walking to their usual turnaround spot at the edge of the property. *I wonder who sent them.*

Chapter 7

The next morning's rehearsal went ahead as scheduled, although the unresolved Civil War issue hung over the proceedings like smoke on a battlefield. A few actors seemed confused and withdrawn, while others responded enthusiastically to Edmund's hands-on, relentlessly demanding directing style.

While Aaron assisted with the running of the rehearsal, Charlotte noted costume change requirements.

Mattie, cast in the role of Beatrice's cousin Hero, appeared sullen and uncooperative in response to Edmund's direction. And on Audrey, he seemed particularly hard, criticizing and belittling her.

Finally, to everyone's relief, he called a twenty-minute break. A few actors left the rehearsal room; others sat on the floor and thumbed through their phones. Audrey, having spotted Charlotte, made a beeline for her, dropped into the seat beside her, and unscrewed the cap to her water bottle.

"This is hard work," she said, "and it's certainly not fun. Nothing like what I expected. He certainly wasn't like this the last time we worked together." She took a long sip and shifted slightly toward Charlotte. "I must apologize to you. I should have trusted your judgment and gone with the American director you recommended."

Charlotte tipped her head in acknowledgment. "It's good of you to say. I wouldn't have dreamed he'd be so authoritarian with the cast. I expected his style would be much more modern, more democratic. Consultative."

"I don't suppose there's any way you could get him to leave? Can his contract be canceled?"

Charlotte shook her head. "We've looked into that, and I don't think so."

Audrey groaned. "If only he could just be made to go away."

"How does the cast feel about his Civil War idea?"

"Some are okay with it, but most either aren't convinced or hate it."

"It's going to cause a huge problem with costumes, I can tell you."

"I wanted to speak to you about that. If it does have to go ahead, I hope you'll be kind and I won't look too ridiculous."

"Of course. That goes without saying."

"Good. Now there's something I wanted to ask you. You've lived here in your bungalow in the grounds for some time, I believe. Have you ever felt, well, unsafe?"

"Not really," Charlotte replied, although it had occurred to her many times that the bungalows were vulnerable. The grounds were open to anyone, day and night; the property wasn't fitted with motion detectors or CCTV cameras; and the old windows on the two bungalows that hadn't been refurbished—hers and the director's—could be opened easily from the outside. "Why do you ask? Has something happened to make you uneasy?"

"No, no. I just think my bungalow isn't very secure. If an intruder wanted to break in, I don't think he'd have too much trouble."

"The windows on your bungalow are new," Charlotte said. "They're sturdy and the glass is tempered. I think you're pretty secure."

"A woman like me who is a bit of a celebrity, a public figure, well, we have to be careful," she said. "I learned a long time ago not to respond too warmly to an attentive fan."

"They can get the wrong idea," agreed Charlotte. "I know. I've seen it."

"It starts small," Audrey said, "and innocently. You don't realize what's happening until it's too late. That's why I don't respond to people on social media. They think you're their best friend and that they have a personal relationship with you. And then the day you don't respond, they take it the wrong way and lash out at you. Or worse."

Charlotte shifted in her seat and leveled a steady gaze at her. "Has something happened? If it has, we need to know."

"I'm not sure. I received a beautiful bouquet yesterday, and at first, I thought nothing of it, really."

"I saw it when it was being delivered," said Charlotte. "It was lovely."

"I'm not sure who sent it. The card just said, 'From an Admirer.'"

"I expect you've had lots of those over the years. Delivered to your dressing rooms and hotels."

"Yes, I have, but I always find it a bit unsettling. I don't like it. I prefer to know who the flowers are from. If the sender doesn't reveal his name, I always assume they're from a married man." She let out a nervous giggle. "But then this morning I received this note."

She reached into the pocket of her jacket and handed over a folded piece of paper. Charlotte unfolded it and read, *I hope you liked the flowers. They were the best I could find but not nearly as beautiful as you.* It was written in a legible, steady hand.

"Oh, dear. When you say you received it, received it how, exactly?"

"I'm not sure what you mean."

"Well, was it hand delivered or did it come in the post?"

"Oh, I see. It was hand delivered."

"Was it left for you here in the theater or at your bungalow?"

"In the theater. It was in my pigeonhole. The A to G slot. You know the ones. In the little room off the lobby where the staff collect their post and messages. Not that there's much of it these days. Post, that is."

"Did it come in an envelope?"

"No, it was just like that. Folded, with my name on it. But it got me thinking. Do you know if any other actresses who performed here received notes like this?"

"No, not that I know of, but you're the first well-known actress we've had in quite some time. I do recall one actor, though, who used to receive rather saucy notes filled with double entendres from middle-aged women, but he just found them amusing and didn't take much notice. Used to read them out loud at lunchtime, and everybody had a laugh. Somehow, though, it's different when the notes are sent to a woman." She handed the note back. "The tone can seem a little more menacing. They can often be taken two ways, although this one does seem harmless and genuine."

"Well, it's probably something and nothing. One doesn't like to make a fuss."

Aaron approached Audrey to tell her the break was over and the director wanted her. With a small sigh, she got to her feet and looked down at Charlotte.

"I wondered if you were able to set up that interview with the local reporter."

As she spoke, Charlotte had a flash of inspiration on who might have sent the flowers.

"I'll ring him right away. Are you free later today for an interview, say four o'clock, if I can set it up? You could use my office."

"I could be available at that time, but why your office? Why don't you send him along to my bungalow?"

"I'm not sure that's a good idea. It would be better if you met on neutral ground. If you're not keen on my office, how about the greenroom? It's not used very often, and I'll tidy it up over lunch and put an 'Occupied' sign on the door so nobody will come in and mess it up this afternoon."

"Audrey!" an impatient Edmund called. "If you wouldn't mind, you're holding us up!"

"Coming!" She turned back to Charlotte. "Fine. The greenroom it is."

*

Fletcher Macmillan, arts reporter for the *Hudson Valley Echo*, kept pace with Charlotte as she escorted him to the greenroom. "Of course, such short notice doesn't give one much time to prepare, but fortunately, I'd already started my research, so I'm well up to speed. Got loads of files and backstories on Audrey. I would have called myself to set up an interview but wanted to give her lots of time to settle in."

"Well, she's just in here," said Charlotte, knocking on the greenroom door and then opening it. The room was used occasionally by actors waiting to go onstage or who had just come off. Charlotte had cleared away water bottles and coffee cups and run a duster over the furniture, and it looked presentable enough. Audrey, seated on the sofa with her legs crossed and turned to one side, looked up as Fletcher entered. He offered her the flowers he was carrying and, after Charlotte had introduced them, sat in the chair facing the sofa. Audrey admired the flowers, then held them up to Charlotte.

"Would you mind putting these in water for me?"

"Of course." She took the flowers and, with a "Right, then, I'll leave you to it," closed the door quietly behind her. On the walk back to her office, she considered the flowers in her hand. The moment Audrey mentioned "reporters," she was sure the starstruck Fletcher Macmillan had sent the presentation bouquet. But if he'd done that, would he show up today with a supermarket offering? When she reached her office, she placed the flowers in water, then picked up the telephone and called A Floral Affair, the flower shop whose name she had seen on the presentation bouquet Aaron had delivered, and asked who had sent the flowers to Audrey Ashley at Jacobs Grand Hotel.

The florist, coolly professional, apologized and said she couldn't possibly reveal that information. The sender had requested anonymity. Charlotte replaced the receiver and, picking up one of the scrap pieces of paper she used for notes to herself, wrote from memory the words on the note Audrey had shown her: *I hope you liked the flowers. They were the best I could find but not nearly as beautiful as you.*

She exhaled slowly and asked herself how she would feel if she received a message containing those words from an unknown person. Perhaps they were meant in a harmless way, but she didn't like the way they made her feel. *As beautiful as you.*

*

As Charlotte and Rupert stepped out of their bungalow for a short before-dinner walk, Ray's marked police car pulled into the parking lot. Ray's suggestion to Harvey that he park the car in front of the building had been welcome, and since its regular overnight appearance, late-night field parties in the grounds, with underage drinking and bonfires, had stopped.

Charlotte's heart flooded with love as she watched him walk toward her. The slanting sun glinted off his metal shirt badge, and she admired the way he carried himself with confidence. He looked fit and handsome in his uniform, and as he got closer, his face broke into a broad smile at the sight of her. When he reached her, he slipped his arm around her waist, pulled her closer, and kissed her. After he and Rupert had exchanged greetings, they stood together for a few minutes on the path.

"We were just going to take a little walk and then do something about dinner," Charlotte said.

"Well, why don't I get changed while you're walking him and then I'll take you out to dinner," Ray suggested. "We haven't gone into town for a while. You choose the restaurant."

"I'd like that," said Charlotte. "I'll think about where I'd like to eat and let you know when we get back from our walk."

As they turned to go, the side door of the hotel opened and Audrey emerged.

"Wait a minute before you go in," said Charlotte. "I should introduce you to our star actress."

"Please don't ask her to join us for dinner," Ray said in a low voice. "I know it would be the nice thing to do, but I really want you all to myself."

Charlotte laughed. "Oh, you are so sweet. Paula's inviting everyone for dinner on the thirtieth anyway, so you'll get to have dinner with her then. That reminds me, I need to talk to her about that."

Audrey had now reached them, and Charlotte introduced Ray to her as the town's chief of police.

Audrey's deep-blue eyes widened slightly as she smiled up at him. She then gave Charlotte a questioning look that Charlotte found hard to read. Was it to do with the flowers and note she'd received from her unknown admirer? Was she signaling Charlotte not to say anything about that? Not that Charlotte would have. If Audrey decided she wanted something reported to the police, she was perfectly capable of doing that herself. "How did your interview with Fletcher Macmillan go?" Charlotte asked.

"Oh, pretty standard. He didn't ask me anything I hadn't been asked before, although I must say, he's terribly earnest."

"I should have warned you about him. He's the most dreadful Anglophile, but he actually writes a pretty good feature story, and he's a stringer for the *New York Times.*" Audrey perked up. "Anyway, Rupert and I were just about to head off for our walk," Charlotte said, "and if you're on your way home, we'll accompany you to your bungalow. There's something I want to talk to you about."

Ray watched them leave and then disappeared into the bungalow he shared with Charlotte.

"About Fletcher Macmillan," said Charlotte. "Did you get a sense that he could have sent you the flowers?"

"He could have, I suppose. He was more than friendly. Almost fawning, I'd say."

"Sounds like him. Anyway, I just wanted to let you know that Paula Van Dusen is giving a dinner party for us at Oakland. It's like a beautiful English country house. You'll love it and feel right at home. You and Maxine will be getting a proper invitation soon, but in the meantime, I hope you'll keep the thirtieth free."

"Oh, that sounds lovely. I'll look forward to it. It'll be one of my last evenings out. I don't go out much when we're in rehearsals, and of course once the play opens, well, your evenings are spoken for, aren't they?" She gave a helpless, what-can-you-do kind of shrug.

"The thing is," said Charlotte, "it will also be a good opportunity for all of us to work on Edmund. To try to get him to change his mind about how he wants to present the play."

"Then I'm definitely in. And Maxine will be too. She spoke to him last night and tried to persuade him not to go ahead with the daft thing, but he's determined that's how he wants it done."

Chapter 8

Charlotte spent the first hour at work the next morning tidying up her office and trying to catch up on her reading. But her thoughts always returned to the costuming for the play if the Civil War version went ahead. As long as she held out hope that Edmund Albright could be persuaded to change his mind, she saw no point in beginning work on the project. And what a lot of work it could turn out to be.

She was starting to think about making another cup of tea when the door opened slowly and Mattie slipped in. Her face was drawn and pale. Charlotte reached out to her.

"Mattie, are you unwell? What's the matter?" Mattie's eyes darted to the open door, so Charlotte shut it firmly and locked it. "Sit down," Charlotte said. "I was just about to make some tea. I'll be right back." She dashed into the little cupboard off the main workroom that housed a small sink, fridge, kettle, and microwave. She filled the kettle, switched it on, and returned to Mattie, who was seated in Aaron's chair, her head resting on her hand.

"What's happened?" Charlotte asked, crouching beside her and resting a hand on her shoulder. "Did somebody say something? Do something?"

Mattie's eyes filled with tears that brimmed in her lower eyelids until one slipped over the edge and rolled down her cheek. She wiped it away with her fingers. "Here," Charlotte said, holding out a box of tissues, "please use these. I hate to see people mopping up tears with their hands." She set the tissues on the desk. "Take a moment to compose yourself and I'll be right back."

She returned with two cups of tea on a small tray. She set the tray on the desk, held out a cup to Mattie, then sat down in her chair. "Tell me what's wrong. When you ran by me on the path, I thought something must have happened and I was worried. Were you coming from Audrey's bungalow? Had you had a row with her?"

Mattie shook her head and whispered, "No."

Charlotte pulled her chair closer. "No. Not Audrey. So Edmund, then, was it?" Mattie nodded miserably. "You had an argument with him?"

"Not really. But I did something really stupid. I asked him to reconsider the casting for the play. I want to play Beatrice. I should play Beatrice. Audrey's too old." Charlotte let that remark go.

"I think you're perfect as Hero. She's described as young, pretty . . . all the things that you are."

"But the whole point of acting is to play someone I'm not! And besides, Hero's such a small part. Maybe forty lines and nothing memorable. Lines like, 'Good Margaret, run thee to the parlor; There shalt thou find my cousin Beatrice . . .' I won't get a chance to show what I can do."

"Sometimes smaller parts pay off in big ways. Think of Judi Dench as Queen Elizabeth I in *Shakespeare in Love*. She was on screen for about eight minutes—eight minutes!—and won an Academy Award for her trouble. So it's not the size of the role that matters. It's what you make of it." Charlotte sighed. "And you could make a lot of this one. Edmund's interpretation of the play could be darker. He's looking at the treatment of women in this play, and the focus of that is Hero. When rehearsals really get going, you'll see this part has much bigger implications than you can see now. There's one more thing I want to tell you that you should find encouraging. Did you know that Helen Mirren once played that part?"

Mattie shook her head slowly. "No, I didn't know that."

"But you really should be having this conversation with Edmund, not me. He's the director."

"I doubt very much I could talk about anything with him now."

"Oh, Mattie, come on. I doubt it's as bad as that. Look, I know you want to get as much experience as you possibly can, but perhaps you should look at what's happening in this situation as part of that experience. Your acting life isn't just about the stage. Just as important is all the other stuff that goes on." She took a sip of tepid tea. "Look, acting is a tough business. You won't always get the parts you want. And then something really awful starts to happen. You realize you're aging out of roles, and the parts that might have been offered to you even a couple of years ago are no longer within your reach. You have to learn to accept these things graciously. It's just part of the job you've chosen to do."

"Well, thanks," muttered Mattie. "That's really cheered me up."

Charlotte smiled. "Sorry. I just want to try to help you put things in perspective. I wish you'd enjoy these days while they're happening, because they won't last forever. One day, you won't be Juliet anymore; you'll be the nurse. Or Lady Capulet. And then the nurse. So make the most of Hero. She's a lovely part, really. With the false accusation of infidelity at the wedding scene, there's huge scope for you to show what you can do, and a good director could pull a brilliant performance out of you. Anyway, there's always discussion about whether Hero and Claudio are really the main plot and Beatrice and Benedick are the subplot. Why not see yourself as the star of the play? Now stand up and let me have a look at you." Mattie did as she was told, and Charlotte gently pinched the side of her loose shirt. "I think you've lost a bit of weight. When we know for sure about the costumes, you'll need a careful fitting."

Mattie sat down again and leveled a direct gaze at Charlotte.

"I hate him. I really do. I didn't know it was possible to hate someone this much."

"Who? Who do you hate?"

"Edmund Albright."

"Because he won't recast the part of Beatrice? But don't you think it was a bit unrealistic of you to ask him to do that? You know that Audrey's been brought over specially to play that part, so why would you think Edmund might give the part to you? He can't. Audrey's got a contract."

"Yes, well, because . . ." Her unsaid words hung between them. And then Charlotte understood.

"Oh, no, you didn't." Mattie lowered her head, and a couple of tears landed on her gray T-shirt. "Did he tell you if you slept with him, he'd give you the Beatrice part?" she asked softly.

"No. He didn't make any promises, and when I thought about it later, he made it quite clear the Beatrice role isn't for me."

"I'm so sorry this has happened. Even though he didn't offer any assurances about the role, I still see what he did as a real abuse of his power, and it makes me so mad that he would take advantage of you like that." Of course, there was nothing new about what Edmund had done, but Charlotte saw Mattie as being more naïve than some young actresses. Some knew exactly what they were doing when they set out to seduce leading actors or directors.

She was prevented from saying more by the sound of someone trying the door handle and finding it locked. A moment later came the sound of a key being inserted into the lock. "That'll be Aaron," said Charlotte, springing out of her chair and running to the door. She opened it smoothly and stepped outside into the corridor in one fluid motion. "Just having a little chat with Mattie," she said. "Can you give us a few minutes? We won't be long, and I'll leave the door open when we're finished."

"Yeah, sure. Is everything all right?"

"It's fine."

"Is she coming back to the rehearsal? Edmund's asking where she is. I came here to ask if you'd seen her."

"She'll be there. Why don't you tell him she's on her way?"

Charlotte returned to her workroom to find Mattie rinsing her face in the little kitchen. "Good," she said. "Sorry, all we have is paper towels, so just blot your face." When Mattie emerged, Charlotte encouraged her to take a few deep, calming breaths to center herself. When she seemed composed, Charlotte said, "It's time for you to head back to rehearsal. Edmund's been asking for you."

"Why is he asking for me? I've finished what I was supposed to do today. The rehearsal schedule doesn't list me for this time period."

"I'll come with you."

They crept into the rehearsal room to find Audrey working with the actor playing Benedick. He was at least ten years younger than she, and as they walked around the space, gesturing at each other or turning their backs, posturing, and waving their scripts, their dynamic seemed artificial. The dialogue between the two characters, meant to be witty and cutting, sounded flat and forced.

Director Edmund Albright sat in a plastic chair, referring to his script, standing occasionally to yell at them. "I know it's early days, but this witty banter between Beatrice and Benedick is meant to be what this play is known for. I'd like some reassurance, please. Could you try to give the impression that eventually it will be at least mildly entertaining?"

Dressed in well-cut blue jeans, sneakers, a shirt with a blue-and-white check, and his light-beige jacket, Edmund rose from his chair every now and then and moved comfortably and easily around the room offering suggestions, asking for specific actions, and sometimes demanding more emotion from the actors.

The rehearsal continued until finally Edmund said to Audrey in front of the rest of the cast, "Why is your acting so wooden this morning? Everything about your timing is off. I know you're capable of so much better, but you're just not giving it to me. I'm tempted to reassign the part of Beatrice to Mattie. And you can play a waiting woman." Several cast members gasped. Audrey tensed and glared at him.

"Why don't you just bugger off back where you came from!" she hissed at him. And then, raising her voice, added, "We'd all be so much better off without you!"

"That's more like it!" Edmund shouted as Audrey tucked the script under her arm and headed for the door.

She wrenched it open, and as the latch clicked into place, she disappeared.

Edmund grinned at the shocked cast members. "Don't worry. A bit old fashioned, I know, but just an old director's trick to light a fire and keep an actress on her toes. She'll be feisty and ready to go when we take up where we left off." He rubbed his hands together. "Right. Let's work on some blocking. Let's be having you, gentlemen, please. I'm looking for Leonato, Don Pedro, Claudio, and Balthasar."

Audrey did not return to the rehearsal room for the rest of the day.

Chapter 9

Charlotte yawned, saved her place with a bookmark, and set the novel on the bedside table. She switched off her reading light and lay in the calm darkness, mulling over the events of the day, including a conversation with Paula Van Dusen about the upcoming dinner party.

The whole *Much Ado* production had got off to what Paula Van Dusen described as "such an unfortunate start" that both she and Charlotte had high hopes that meeting socially would settle everyone; help them see one another's points of view through fresh, sympathetic eyes; and restore a civilized calm to the situation. And then Paula had mentioned that the board had discussed Edmund's proposed Civil War theme and that she would share their thoughts at dinner. Despite Charlotte's pleas, Paula had refused to tell her what approach the board had decided to take. "I promised the board members that we'd let everyone know at the same time," she said. "That's the only fair way to do this. It would be inappropriate for you to know before other people, like the director and lead actress, who are just as involved as you are. As much as I'd like to tell you—and in light of our friendship, you know I wish I could—I can't, and I'm afraid you're just going to have to be patient."

"No more of my gin and tonic for you, then," Charlotte had replied easily, smoothing over the awkwardness of the moment and the disappointment she felt.

"And you'll have to wait to hear until after the starter," Paula had added. "One never discusses business until after the soup or salad. My father-in-law taught me that years ago, and it's a rule I always follow at my dinner parties. Social niceties first, then business."

As Ray lay sleeping beside her, Charlotte contemplated various dinner party scenarios and what might happen. Finally she, too, closed her eyes and drifted off into a fitful sleep.

In what seemed like just a few minutes but was actually a couple of hours, the ringing of Ray's cell phone awakened her. She felt his body position shift as he reached for it, then heard him speaking softly as he got out of bed. "Oh, no," said Charlotte. "What is it?"

"Report of a prowler at Audrey's."

He straightened up, lifted Rupert onto the bed, and grinned as Charlotte put her arm around him and they settled in for a cuddle. Ray could think of somebody who loved late-night callouts enormously, and he reckoned that if Rupert had a phone of his own, he'd make the calls himself just to get Ray out of the way so he could have Charlotte all to himself.

Ray let himself out of the house, locked the door behind him, switched on his flashlight, and—holding the light in his left hand, his right hand on the gun on his hip— headed down the path to Audrey's bungalow. A light was on in the director's bungalow, but it was switched off as he passed. Making a mental note to ask Edmund Albright if he'd heard or seen anything suspicious, he continued on to Audrey's. After performing a careful check around the house, he knocked on Audrey's door. "Police," he called out. The door was opened by a short woman with attractive gray hair worn in a soft pageboy style. "Oh," said Ray, "I was expecting to see Audrey. You must be . . ."

"I'm her sister," said the woman. "Maxine Kaminski. You'd better come in."

"Can you tell me what's going on here?" Ray asked as she led him into the sitting room. "And where's your sister? Is she all right?"

"I think so. She's in her room. She felt poorly and went to lie down. She said you could go in and talk to her if you needed to."

"Why don't you tell me what happened?" Ray asked. "What did you hear? Did you see anything?"

"Nothing. I was asleep. Dead to the world, I was, and the next thing I know, Audrey's shaking me awake and telling me there's someone outside. I didn't hear anything, but she was obviously upset, so I got up, and she phoned the police, and then she felt a bit wobbly so she went to lie down, and you arrived."

"Maxine?" came a faint voice from the next room. "Who are you talking to? Is the police officer here?" Maxine excused herself and walked to the doorway of the bedroom. "Yes, he's just asking a few questions." Audrey said something Ray didn't quite catch. Maxine retraced the few steps back to the sitting room and sat down.

"She wants to know if there's anything you want to ask her," she said.

Ray stood up. "No. I'll let her get some rest now. I've had a look around outside, and there doesn't seem to be a sign of anybody, but it's hard to tell in the darkness. I'll send someone around in the morning to take another look."

*

Charlotte was swirling something around in a pot when Ray arrived home. "Cooking? At his hour?" he asked.

"You know I have trouble sleeping when you're out on a night call, so I'm making a cup of cocoa. It's what we Brits do when we can't sleep. Want one?"

"Love one."

Charlotte opened the fridge door, took out the milk carton, and added more milk to the pot. She handed the container to Ray to put away and continued gently moving the pot over the heat. "Well?" she asked, not looking at him.

"I didn't see Audrey. Her sister answered the door. The sister'd been asleep and didn't hear or see anything. Audrey called the police and then went to bed."

"Do you think someone was hanging around the place?"

"I'm not sure. I didn't see anything to indicate there is." Ray unfastened his police duty belt and set it on a chair. "I'll remind Harvey to get the bushes around the bungalows cut back so it won't be as easy for someone to hide in them." Charlotte made a paste of cocoa, sugar, and milk in two cups; poured the hot milk into each; gave them a noisy stir; and handed a cup to Ray. They sat at the kitchen table, Charlotte in her dressing gown and Ray in his uniform, their hands cupped around their mugs of comforting cocoa.

"Should I take Rupert out?" Ray asked when they were finished. Rupert looked up at him and waggled his bottom, so Ray opened the door, and the two disappeared into the night. They returned a few minutes later, and Ray locked the door, turned off the light, and joined Charlotte in bed.

They held each other in the darkness, and as their breathing quieted and slowed, Charlotte's sleepy voice broke through the stillness. "Ray?"

"Mhmm."

"Did you check to make sure the stove was turned off?"

Chapter 10

As the sun slipped behind the Catskill Mountains, filling the sky with a scattering of pink light, the burgundy Rolls-Royce meandered along the two-lane highway toward Oakland, Paula Van Dusen's country estate. Set in beautifully tended, award-winning lawns and gardens, the house was protected by a massive black wrought-iron gate that swung smoothly and silently open to admit the Rolls-Royce ferrying the dinner guests.

Audrey Ashley gazed out the window and exchanged a warm, knowing smile with her sister as the car made its way along the driveway, past beds of colorful late summer perennials in full bloom. Edmund Albright, sitting beside the other window, had remained silent throughout the twenty-minute journey. Except for the occasional glance out the window at the passing greenery, his eyes had remained fixed on the back of the chauffeur's head.

The sprawling late Victorian house, with its gables and chimneys that provided a varied and detailed roof line, was built of locally quarried gray stone. The car slowed to a stop in front of the main door, where Paula Van Dusen waited to welcome her guests.

Wearing a cocktail sheath of midnight-blue lace, her dark hair arranged in a neat chignon and her face beautifully made up, she held out her hand and greeted each arrival by name.

"Audrey, lovely to see you. Hello, Edmund. And Maxine. Welcome to Oakland. Shall we go in?"

Chatting in a relaxed and engaging manner, she led her guests through an immense, high-ceilinged entry hall with black-and-white flooring and down a corridor to a large sitting room at the back of the house. The French doors that led to the terrace stood open, letting in the last of the dying light as the pinks of sunset were absorbed by the deep purples of twilight. Standing by the fireplace, drinks in hand, were Charlotte and Ray. Charlotte, wearing a becoming little black dress and pearl stud earrings, smiled at the new arrivals.

"Now let me introduce everybody," Paula said. "Unfortunately, Harvey's wife was unable to join us this evening, but we're happy that his secretary, Nancy Hargreaves, agreed to come in her stead." As Harvey's name was mentioned, he stood up, but Nancy remained primly seated, back erect and eyes alert. The gray suit she wore to the office had given way to a navy-blue, calf-length dress in a nondescript, synthetic fabric.

"Now then," said Paula. "Where are Roger and Sonja?"

"Here, Paula." A couple who appeared to be in their late fifties or early sixties stepped through the French doors. They had that air of authoritative confidence about them associated with expensive grooming and well-tailored, classic clothes with deep pockets. "Just enjoying the remains of the day," said the man.

Paula introduced the theater people to the couple.

"And I'm delighted that Roger and Sonja Harrison were able to join us tonight. Both of them serve on the theater board with me and are eager to meet our new director and lead actress.

"Now, Roger," Paula continued, "would you be kind enough to give me a hand with the drinks?" She made her way to the drinks table and asked over her shoulder, "Audrey, what can I get you?"

Before Audrey could respond, Maxine answered for both of them. "She'll have a small vodka and tonic, no ice, and I'll have a tonic with ice, please."

A moment later, a young woman entered the room with a tray of canapés. Audrey shook her head as the woman approached her, but Maxine accepted a pale-blue napkin and helped herself to a small mushroom vol-au-vent and a mini quiche.

The conversation started off strained and awkward, but civil. Audrey's eyes flickered from Ray to Charlotte and back again, narrowing slightly. She said something in a low voice to her sister, who then turned to speak to Edmund and Paula as Audrey joined Ray and Charlotte.

"Well, hello again," she said brightly to Ray. "Hello, Charlotte. Paula certainly has a lovely home, doesn't she? I especially like the fence and gate! No unwanted prowlers here!" Ray smiled and Audrey gave him a sly look before moving on to exchange a few words with the Harrison couple. A few minutes later, dinner was announced, and they all moved into the oak-paneled dining room. When they were seated, the server placed a bowl of steaming tomato-and-basil soup in front of each diner and then circled the table pouring wine. Gradually, the din of congenial conversation filled the room as the guests relaxed and almost began to enjoy themselves.

The server removed the soup bowls and set an entrée in front of everyone. Knowing where Paula was now going to steer the conversation, Charlotte braced herself. One way or another, someone would be going home unhappy.

"Now then. Might I have your attention, please?" Paula Van Dusen tapped her water glass with her knife. The room fell silent, and all eyes turned expectantly toward her. "I think it best if I just get right to it. Our new director, Edmund Albright"—she tipped her head in his direction—"arrived with an unusual proposal that caught us all off guard: that the upcoming production of *Much Ado About Nothing* be performed as a Civil War piece, specifically set in the North. There was resistance, if not outright opposition, to the idea among some of the cast and crew, as well as board members, but because of the way Edmund's contract is worded, the board has no authority to override his artistic decision. Two of our board members are with us tonight, but I can assure you all the rest have been consulted. So speaking as the chairperson of the board, it falls to me to say that after much discussion and consideration, we have decided . . ."

Edmund leaned forward while Audrey rested her elbow on the table and, after glancing nervously at her sister, covered her mouth with the tips of her fingers. Sensing what was coming, Charlotte held her breath.

". . . that we are giving our approval for the Civil War production."

Edmund's face creased into a big grin as he exclaimed, "Yes!"

Roger Harrison picked up where Paula left off. "We liked the idea of creating something fresh and new. We think this production will attract a lot of attention—especially from the New York media—get people talking, and really put the theater on the map. We expect it will bring in bigger audiences later into the season.

"But we didn't make the decision alone. We polled an online Shakespeare course, and we spoke to local educators. Everyone is quite excited about the idea, and I must admit, so are we. To be honest, at first we were heartily against the idea, but we did come 'round to seeing it as something we should try. Especially since next year is the four hundredth anniversary of Shakespeare's death, and theater groups around the world are going to show how relevant and timeless his body of work really is."

"It's all about modernizing the play," said Sonja Harrison. "Well, modernizing it into the nineteenth century."

"I've just had this terrific idea," said Edmund. "Let's have the two brothers, Don Pedro and Don John, as soldiers fighting on opposite sides during the war. One for the North, one for the South."

"Well, that'll be for you to work out," said Paula. "Now I know there are budget concerns," she continued, anticipating Charlotte's protests, "so we're allocating from our reserve funds what we think is an adequate amount for costumes. We don't think whole new sets will be required, but appropriate changes can be made to the existing ones.

"However, time is not our friend here. The production will have to be put together quickly so we can keep to our schedule and open on time. And we're going to need new posters and other advertising materials. But all in all, we're quite excited by the idea. It will, however, require everyone working together, so I hope all of you will accept our decision and really get on board with the project. We had some delays when we lost the previous director, and now it has to be full steam ahead for everybody involved."

Audrey sank back in her chair, gazing at her hands, fingers intertwined, resting on the edge of the table. She pushed her plate away, and Maxine, seated beside her, stretched her hand along the tablecloth and grasped her sister's.

"What do you think, Audrey?" Paula asked gently.

Audrey raised head and leveled a steady gaze at Edmund, sitting across the table from her. "I've been against this daft idea from the beginning, and I certainly wasn't expecting to hear this tonight. I thought we were here to see if we could talk some sense into Edmund, to make him see how disastrous this is going to be, and frankly, I'm feeling betrayed. I never would have agreed to perform this play, at this theater, had I known the production was going to be nontraditional."

"We acknowledge that the situation hasn't been handled well," Paula said. "Edmund should have proposed his idea to the board before dropping it on the cast with no warning."

"Yes," said Edmund, glancing first at Paula, then facing Audrey's belligerent stare. "And I certainly should have discussed it with you. I apologize."

As the uncertain mood lifted, conversation resumed, and the diners returned to their plates. Audrey, however, left hers untouched, and eventually, forks were laid down and a server appeared to clear the table.

"Now we've got something typically American for dessert tonight," announced Paula. "Old-fashioned apple pie!"

Audrey shook her head as the server placed a generous slice of apple pie—its latticed crust golden and flaky, with warm, cinnamon-laced chunky apple filling oozing onto the plate—in front of each diner. It was accompanied by scoops of homemade French vanilla ice cream and slices of locally made, mature cheddar cheese.

When the dessert course was finished, the group moved back to the sitting room, where a coffee service had been set up. Ray passed around cups of coffee, and Charlotte followed with a selection of liqueurs. Audrey allowed herself a small brandy under Maxine's disapproving eye.

Eventually, the evening wound down, and the guests made their way to the front door. After thanking their hostess, they headed to their vehicles, and the little convoy set off down the driveway.

"Are you and Aaron going to be okay with those costumes?" Ray asked Charlotte as they turned onto the highway in the red glow of the Rolls-Royce's taillights.

"We'll just have to be. I'll meet with Edmund to go over everything, but we can make a few new dresses, rent the men's Civil War uniforms as Aaron suggested, and perhaps adapt existing costumes for minor characters. I think Aaron's going to be excited."

"Audrey didn't seem thrilled."

"I'll talk to her. We can make it work. Possibly even to her advantage." In the greenish light from the dashboard, she glanced at Ray's profile. "I wonder, though, if it was really a Civil War theme Edmund was after or if he just wanted to get his own way. If what he really wanted was to win. To make a point with Audrey, for some reason."

In the back seat, Harvey Jacobs and Nancy remained silent the entire journey. As Ray dropped Nancy off at her home, he mentioned that several lights were on upstairs.

"Oh, my niece is staying with me," Nancy said. "I've reminded her a thousand times about turning off lights in empty rooms, but she isn't as mindful of that as I am. Of course, she doesn't have to pay the electricity bill."

*

Audrey, Maxine, and Edmund Albright climbed out of the Rolls-Royce and stood for an uncertain moment in an awkward cluster watching Barnes drive off. Before anyone could say anything, Ray's police car arrived, and Charlotte hopped out of the front seat and joined them.

"Ray wants us all to walk home together," she said. "He especially wants to make sure Audrey and Maxine get home safely." Her presence released some of the tension between Edmund and the sisters, and together, they walked toward the path that led to the bungalows, where Ray caught up with them. After seeing Charlotte safely inside, he rejoined the other three, and with his flashlight's bright beam guiding them, they continued on. Edmund was next, and finally, Ray escorted Maxine and Audrey to their bungalow. He held out his hand for their key, unlocked the door, switched on the kitchen light, then checked both bedrooms. When he was satisfied the bungalow was empty, he opened the door and the two women entered. Audrey brushed past him and headed straight for her bedroom.

"Well, good night," said Ray, handing the door key to Maxine. "Be sure to lock the door behind me. Let's hope no one is disturbed tonight."

He let himself into his and Charlotte's bungalow a few minutes later and, loosening his tie, reached for Rupert's leash to take him out for his last little walk before bed. They strolled back along the path, almost as far as the director's bungalow, then returned home. The night was still and peaceful, and Ray hoped it would remain that way so everyone got a good night's sleep. He suspected the next few days at the theater were going to be busy and filled with more drama than the players might wish.

He let Rupert and himself into the house to find Charlotte changed into a pair of soft cotton pajama bottoms and a pink T-shirt, curled up on the sofa, waiting for them.

"Can I get you anything?" he asked her. "Nightcap?"

"No, I've had enough to drink, thanks." Rupert jumped up on the sofa, and she wrapped her arms around him. "I'm knackered. I've had enough for one night. Luckily, Aaron's done some costume sketches, so at least we have a starting point. Now that we know for sure what direction we're going in, we've got to get our skates on."

"Skates on?"

"It's an English expression. Get going. Get on with things."

"Oh, right."

Ray checked one last time to make sure the door was locked and turned off the lights.

Chapter 11

"Well, I must say, Charlotte, you're a bit of a dark horse," said Audrey the next morning when they passed each other in the hotel parking lot. Charlotte was on her way into the hotel to review Aaron's sketches, and Audrey, apparently having finally found something palatable for her breakfast in the cafeteria, was just coming out.

"What do you mean?"

"Not telling me you're involved with the dishy policeman. Although, I've seen him around here often enough, I should have realized."

Charlotte shrugged. "Didn't I say? Sorry. I guess I don't really like talking about my personal life."

Audrey gave a fluttery laugh. "Well, you're forgiven."

As she started to walk off, Charlotte placed a gentle hand on her forearm. "Audrey, just a moment. You and I need to have a chat about your costumes, and the sooner the better. The thing is, I've given your costume requirements a lot of thought, and I believe we can make this situation work to your advantage. We make sure you look fabulous, and then, if the production is as easy to promote because of the Civil War angle as everyone seems to think it will be, you'll get a lot more attention. After all, look what playing a Civil War beauty did for Vivian Leigh's career, and she was English too."

Audrey's blue eyes sparkled. "You might be right. I should have been more open-minded and given poor Edmund a chance. I did say some awful things to him. As difficult it would be for me, I wonder if an apology would be a good idea."

"I think that would be helpful. If both of us show willing, we'll probably get more done, and everything will be a whole lot easier. We're really under a lot of time pressure now. Look, Aaron's done some concept sketches. Why don't you come to the office with me and take a look at them? And after you've reviewed them, we'll see when Edmund's available to discuss your costumes."

"Sounds good."

Minutes later, Charlotte opened a folder and spread Aaron's sketches over the worktable. "We can modify anything to suit you," she explained as Audrey pored over them.

"This neckline could be a little lower," said Audrey, pointing at one, "and I'm not sure about this skirt. It doesn't seem full enough. But it's hard to tell without seeing and feeling the fabric."

"We haven't got any swatches yet, but we will," Charlotte assured her. "And trust me, the end results will be flattering."

When Audrey had finished examining the sketches, Charlotte replaced them in their folder and snapped it shut.

"What do you think?"

"I like them."

"Good. Now let's see if we can find Edmund." She picked up her desk telephone and dialed the four-digit extension to the director's office. There was no response. "I'll try the bungalow." Again, no response. "He might be in the shower, or he could have gone out, I suppose," she said as she replaced the receiver. "We'll try him again later, although I was really hoping we could get on with this."

"Maybe he slept in after last night. Perhaps we should just go over and knock on his door. See if he's home."

"I don't really like when people just pop in on me, so I don't like doing that to other people."

"Well, suit yourself, but I'm going over there. As much as it pains me to do so, I really must apologize for certain things I said to him in the heat of the moment and I'd like to get it over with. It would be easier for me if you'd come with me."

"Oh, all right," said Charlotte. She gathered up the folder of sketches and locked the door, and then they retraced their steps across the parking lot.

"Rupert not with you this morning?" Audrey remarked as they passed Charlotte's bungalow.

"Ray had him out for quite a long walk earlier and tired him out. He seemed content in his basket, so I'm letting him have a nice lie-in this morning."

"Maybe Edmund's having a lie-in too."

"I hope not. That's why I'm really not comfortable dropping in on people unannounced. Or they may not be properly dressed."

"Oh, well, we're here now," said Audrey when they reached the director's bungalow. "We might as well give it a try." She climbed the three steps and knocked on the door. When there was no answer, Charlotte checked her watch.

"It's not quite ten. It might be a bit too early." She joined Audrey on the top step and peered through the little window in the door into the kitchen.

She tried the door handle, and when it turned, she pushed the door open and entered.

"Hello?" she called. "Edmund, it's me, Charlotte Fairfax. Audrey's with me. Are you here? We need to speak to you."

There was no response, so she entered the kitchen.

"Maybe this wasn't such good idea after all," came a whispery voice from behind her. "It's rather creepy. I think we should leave."

And then Charlotte smelled it. A pungent, rusty smell, like a jar of old pennies that had been left out in the rain.

The unmistakable smell of blood. Heart pounding, afraid but driven to look, she inched toward the source of the smell and stood in the doorway between the kitchen and sitting room. Pale-beige light filtering through the drawn curtains cast the room into semidarkness, but she could see well enough to make out the body of Edmund Albright sprawled on the sofa, legs outstretched at odd, awkward angles and head lolling to his left. He wore the same beige trousers and blue shirt he'd worn to the dinner party, but both garments were now heavily stained with dark-brown splotches. His arms flopped by his side, his left hand resting palm up and the fingers of his right hand loosely curled around a handgun.

"Oh, God," screamed Audrey over Charlotte's shoulder. "He's killed himself. Oh, I never should have . . ." She covered her mouth with her hand and gagged. "The smell." She twisted away and escaped through the kitchen, the screen door banging shut in her wake. Charlotte, too, overcome by waves of nausea, took a few backward steps into the kitchen and then to the fresh air and ordinariness of outside. Relieved to be no longer within sight of Edmund's pallid, gray face, she groped in her pocket for her phone while Audrey hovered on the path.

"Yes," she panted in reply to Ray's question. "Yes! I'm absolutely sure he's dead. He's well beyond help, believe me."

While they waited for Ray to arrive, she returned to the kitchen. She knew not to touch anything but thought she could at least look. The counter seemed to have been wiped down. A few documents lay scattered on the kitchen table beside a teapot. She peered at them and recognized production notes for *Much Ado*, a production that could now be in doubt. *He must have been working on those documents while he had a cup of tea*, she thought. *But where's the cup he used?* There were no dishes in the sink, so it could have been washed and put away. She glanced back at the teapot, and then, setting the folder of Aaron's drawings on the table and covering her hands with a tea towel, she opened a drawer and removed a spoon. Placing the edge of the spoon under the lid of the teapot, being careful not to touch the knob on the lid, she lifted it up and peered inside, then slowly let the lid fall back into place. She put the spoon back in the drawer and stepped outside to find Ray talking to Audrey, who was gesturing toward the bungalow, while another police officer prepared to unspool a roll of yellow police tape to cordon off the area.

"Oh, the poor man," Audrey wailed. "The gun's right there on the sofa beside him. Killing himself like that. It's just too awful."

"That's not for you to decide," Ray told her. "The state police will be here soon to start their investigation, and they'll determine if it was suicide. Now how about we have Sergeant Davenport here"—he gestured at the officer who had finished tying the police tape to a sapling—"walk you home? You shouldn't be alone right now. Is your sister available to look after you? We'll come back later to take your statement."

Audrey nodded, her face set in a mask of numb disbelief. Ray tipped his head at Phil Davenport, and the two set off.

"And you," Ray said, wrapping a comforting arm around Charlotte. "Are you all right? I'll take you home as soon as Phil gets back. Are you okay to wait here with me? I can't leave the scene." She nodded, and they stood without speaking, her head resting on his shoulder, for the few minutes it took Phil to see Audrey home and then return.

"You take over here, Phil. Won't be long," Ray directed.

Once home, Charlotte sank gratefully into her sofa. She leaned forward and rested her elbows on her knees, covering her eyes with her hands as if trying to block out what she'd just seen. Ray sat beside her and rested a hand on her back. "What brought the two of you to his bungalow this morning?" he asked gently.

"We wanted to get started on this costume business. We needed his opinion on the concept sketches Aaron had done." She straightened up with a startled expression. "Oh! I must have left them there. On his kitchen counter, maybe. Or table. Can you get them for me?" Ray assured her he would. "Anyway, we rang Edmund's office, but there was no answer, so we tried the bungalow. Thought he might have slept in after last night, so we decided to walk over. It was more Audrey's idea than mine, really. I don't like just popping in on people, but she talked me into it. Said she owed him an apology, wanted to get it over with, and asked me to go with her." She leaned back into the sofa. "Shouldn't you have taken a look at him?"

"No. There's nothing I can do there. Me not going in means one less person walking through the scene before the forensics people process it."

Chapter 12

"I don't want to leave you, but the state police will be here soon, and I've got to be there to meet them," Ray said a few minutes later. "Will you be all right?"

"Yes. I'll be fine. You go. I've got calls to make. Harvey should be informed, hopefully before the police arrive."

He kissed her good-bye, holding her for a few extra seconds. When he had gone, she picked up the house phone and dialed Harvey's apartment. After speaking to his wife, she hung up and called his office. When Nancy answered, Charlotte told her what had happened, that the local police were on scene, and that the state police had been notified and were expected any minute. "So just be aware, there's going to be a lot of police activity for the next few days," she said. Then she added, "Oh, and Fletcher Macmillan will probably be sniffing around soon." She ended the call and moved on to the next one.

"Paula? It's bad news, I'm afraid." After describing the discovery of Edmund's body, she added, "Of course, we're going to need another director, and fast. Do you suppose Wade Radcliffe is still available?" She listened for a moment and then said, "Lunch? Good idea. At Oakland? In an hour? Right. I'll be ready."

After changing into a sunny yellow top, black skinny jeans, and a pair of black loafers, Charlotte walked Rupert to the hotel parking lot where Barnes was waiting for her with the Van Dusen Rolls-Royce. She lifted Rupert onto the back seat, climbed in after him, and they set off.

The winding road led past farms with roadside displays of locally grown squash, beets, tomatoes, cucumbers, and corn for sale. Banks of gold-and-purple wild flowers flanked the highway, and the trees were showing the signs of heat exhaustion that would lead to next month's change in the color of their foliage. Charlotte sank back in the luxurious leather seats, relishing the ease and comfort in the midst of all the turmoil.

Paula was waiting for her on the steps of the mansion with her own corgi, a red-and-white puppy called Coco, at her heels. She handed Coco's leash to Barnes and indicated Charlotte should do the same with Rupert's. "Just let them have a nice little run in the garden, Barnes, and when you've tired them out, bring them 'round to the kitchen door and make sure there's water for them."

Paula and Charlotte made their way quickly and silently through the great hall to the sitting room at the rear of the house where Paula mixed a gin and tonic, added a slice of lime, and handed it to Charlotte. She mixed her own drink, then sat close to Charlotte on the sofa.

"How absolutely dreadful for you," she said. "Are you sure you're all right?"

"I'm fine. But I've just realized what a good idea it was to come here, to get away from . . ." As the sentence trailed off, Paula gave her a reassuring hug.

"When you're ready," Paula said, "I'd really like to hear about it."

She listened intently while Charlotte described, step by step and in great detail, everything that had happened that morning.

"And what did he look like, if you don't mind my asking?" Paula said, looking at Charlotte over the rim of her glass. "I'm just curious. I've never come across a dead body before. I suspect few people have."

"He was slumped over to his left, and it was obvious from the blood stains on his clothes, mainly on his shirt, that something terrible had happened. The curtains were closed, but from the available light in the room, I could see that there was a gun in his hand, so it looks like he died of a gunshot wound. I didn't go in the room. Just looked from the doorway. Didn't want to disturb anything." Charlotte spared her the description of the smell.

"And do the police think it was suicide?"

"I don't know what they think. They've just started the investigation, but that's something they'll consider, I guess."

"What did you think?"

"Well, I'm not an expert, of course, and I don't want to speculate, but that's what it looked like. I'm sure the police will determine what happened with all their forensics testing. Ballistics and gunpowder residue and all the other CSI stuff you see on TV. But I can't think of any reason why he would do such a thing. He seemed happy to be working here and excited about the possibilities of the new production. Especially after last night, when you gave him the board's blessing to go ahead." She wiped some condensation off her glass with her napkin. "And where on earth would he get a gun?"

"Oh, they're not hard to come by," said Paula.

"Well, maybe not for an American who lives here, but surely you must need to know how to go about getting one or at least where to go," said Charlotte. "I wouldn't know where to start, and I've lived here for ten years, although I suppose if I were really desperate, I could grab Ray's. But I wouldn't know to use it.

"Anyway, I've never wanted a gun, or even thought about it, really, but all the same. So how would Edmund know how to get a gun? He'd only been in the country five minutes. And besides, guns just aren't something an English person planning to commit suicide would think of."

"No? What would they think of?"

"Hanging would be my guess."

"Okay, so setting the gun aside for now, you discovered the body when you went to his bungalow," Paula mused, "when he wasn't expecting you, and you weren't even sure if he was home."

"I know. I got swept along with what Audrey wanted. She said she wanted to apologize to him for some things she'd said. I don't know if she was referring to the things she said to him at rehearsal, like telling him to sod off, or if she'd said other things to him, in private."

"I've been thinking about Audrey and Edmund," said Paula, "and it seems to me something personal must have been going on between them back in England. There's a history there, don't you think? Why else would she want him to come out here and direct her in this play? No, not 'want him to,'" she corrected herself, "*insist* that he did. We had a perfectly good director lined up, and she invoked the director approval clause in her contract."

"They've worked together before," Charlotte reminded her, "and I think she has so much riding on the success of this play she wanted a director she could trust to make her look her best. And then he dropped that bombshell about the Civil War theme, and she was very unhappy with him."

They had finished their drinks, and Paula suggested they move into the dining room. "We'll talk about where we go from here over lunch."

Two place settings graced by a small centerpiece of apricot-pink roses in a silver bowl had been arranged at one end of the table.

"Lovely roses, Paula," Charlotte said, leaning over the table and inhaling their subtle fragrance.

"Yes, they are. They're called Ambridge Roses. Poor Ned's had a terrible time with his roses this summer. Always going on about the black spot, and in the most mournful way, as if he's about to burst into tears." She laughed. "He takes great pride in the Oakland rose gardens, and we're so lucky to have him. He grows some roses that you just don't see anywhere else. Those"— she nodded at the centerpiece—"are his particular favorite this summer. He planted lavender bushes near them because he likes the combination of colors."

They took their seats, and Charlotte admired the table setting.

"Do you always eat lunch like this?" she asked as she unfolded her napkin and placed it on her lap.

"No. Only when I'm lucky enough to have someone like you join me. If I'm on my own, sometimes I skip lunch altogether or have a tray with something light in the sitting room or my office," Paula said. "But this is much nicer, so I'm glad you're here, even though the circumstances are so unpleasant."

"Me too."

"With so much going on, we've got a lot to talk about."

A server appeared with two small Caesar salads and a bottle of white wine. "You can just leave that here," said Paula, nodding at the wine bottle. "We'll pour it ourselves." She filled their glasses, and the server set down their salads.

"I rang Roger Harrison as soon as you called me," Paula said, "to get his opinion on what the board should do. I know what I thought, but just wanted to make sure I had support. We think the production must go ahead."

"I agree. Absolutely it must."

"So I called Wade Radcliffe to see if he's available to direct this production, and fortunately, he's still willing to take on the project."

"What about Audrey and the director approval business that brought Edmund Albright here in the first place?"

"I'm sure she'll approve Wade now. And if she doesn't, we'll have to find a way to get her out of the contract. But I'm sure it won't come to that. She's a professional, and she'll want to get as much mileage out of this as she can. She'll also understand that enough time has been wasted and we've got to move forward."

"Yes, as Harvey said a while ago about this production, we're burning daylight. Oh, well, so much for Aaron's Civil War sketches. I guess Audrey's going to get her way after all, and we're back to a traditional look. But she seemed to be coming around to the idea."

"Well, that's good." Before Charlotte could ask her what she meant, the server reappeared and stood silently behind them, with her back to an elaborately carved oak sideboard with dozens of silverware drawers. When Paula indicated they had finished their salads, the server removed the plates and left the room. She returned a few minutes later, her hands wrapped in white tea towels, carrying two piping hot plates. She set a plate—each with a small portion of grilled salmon in dill sauce on a bed of rice with sautéed red-and-yellow peppers and carrots—before each woman.

"This looks delicious," said Charlotte, picking up her fork. "Now tell me. What did you mean when you said, 'That's good?'"

"Roger and I are of the opinion"—Paula paused to take a sip of wine—"that there are good reasons to continue with the Civil War theme—the publicity it will attract, to give the cast some continuity, and to honor the memory of Edmund Albright, to name three—so we want it done that way."

"And have you told Wade this?"

"Well, no, I'm not a theater person. I don't really have the expertise to discuss it with him. I don't know what it would involve."

"Oh, no!" groaned Charlotte. "You want me to tell him."

"Well, wouldn't that make the most sense? You'll be working closely with him, and since you're essentially running the company now, we thought you should be the one to tell him."

"But Paula, do you realize how difficult it will be for Wade to present another director's interpretation of this play? Each director sets the mood and finds different themes within the script." She emphasized her words with an open hand gesture. "Simon's version was going to be light and comedic. And then Edmund was going for a darker concept. He wanted to focus on the gender politics." She shook her head. "You know what they say about a camel being a horse designed by a committee? This will be the third director attached to this production, and I can't imagine what the end result is going to look like. Is there anything else that can go wrong with it, I wonder?" She sliced a juli-enned carrot in half. "Tell you what. I'll break the news to Wade if you break the news about Edmund to Brian Pren-tice. He should know what's happened, and it would be bet-ter coming from us, before it makes the British newspapers."

Brian Prentice, the company's previous star actor, had opted out of his contract on medical grounds to return to England for treatment and been replaced by Audrey. Hav-ing had a long, successful career in British theater, he knew everybody, and because of his affiliation with the Catskills Shakespeare Theater Company, Charlotte knew he'd be more than interested to hear about Edmund.

"We'll telephone Brian right after lunch," Paula said. "Now I hope you've saved a bit of room. There's raspberry and white chocolate cheesecake. We'll each have just a sliver."

Charlotte laughed. "A sliver. I knew a woman once who ate a whole cake, a sliver at a time."

"It wasn't you, was it?"

"I'll never tell."

"What kind of cake was it?"

"Lemon drizzle."

*

When they'd finished dessert, Paula asked for a tea tray to be delivered to her ground-floor office. The room had once been her mother-in-law's morning room. Back then, it was paneled with mahogany, dark and closed in with heavy furniture and massively tall plants. Now it was bright and spacious. Paula's desk was positioned near the tall windows to make the most of the natural light that poured in. A butterscotch-colored leather sofa, part of a comfortable seating area, took up a corner of the room, and it was from here that Paula conducted most of her business. One wall was taken up with a whiteboard, now blank.

When Paula and Charlotte were settled, with a tea tray on the low table in front of them, Paula dialed Brian in London. He answered on the third ring and seemed really pleased to hear from her. "Charlotte's here with me," said Paula, "and I'd like to put you on speakerphone so we can all be part of the conversation. Is that all right with you?" A moment later, Brian's deep booming bass voice filled the room.

"Charlotte, love, how are you?"

"Fine, thanks, Brian. You sound well."

"Oh, I am. I've finished the treatment, and it's gone well. Doctors are very pleased. Feeling fine."

"Good," said Paula. "Brian, I'm afraid we've had some bad news here at the theater company, and we wanted you to hear it from us before you read about it in the British press."

"Sod those buggers!"

"Yes, well, it's about Edmund Albright. We had brought him in as a replacement director for Simon Dyer."

Because Brian had invested in the theater school project, Charlotte had notified him of Simon's departure and let him know that his investment would be returned when the project's business and legal affairs were wrapped up.

"Yes, I'd heard that. He can be a bit of a loose cannon, young Edmund, but by all accounts, he gets spectacular results. What's happened? Is he not working out?"

Paula and Charlotte exchanged a quick glance before Charlotte responded.

"It's not that. Worse, much worse. He died last night, and well, there's no easy way to say this. Gunshot. Looks like suicide."

"But that's impossible!" Brian said after a pause. "He rang me about the job just before he went out there. Keen as mustard, he was. Had come up with the idea of an American Civil War backdrop. Made it sound so damned exciting, I would have leapt at the chance to play Leonato. Why would he do such a bloody fool thing? He was starting to get noticed. He was in talks with the RSC, and it looked like he was in line for an artistic director's position. They just wanted him to get a bit more experience, and everybody agreed doing this play in America would give him exactly the credentials he needed. It was the perfect career step for him at this time. He had high hopes for good notices in the *New York Times*." Charlotte and Paula exchanged puzzled glances. "It doesn't make sense," Brian concluded. "I don't believe for a minute he committed suicide. There's got to be some mistake."

"Well, the police haven't officially ruled it a suicide," Charlotte said. "That's just what it looked like."

"What it looked like," Brian repeated. "You mean, you . . ."

"Yes," said Charlotte. "I found the body."

"Well, I suppose things could have been going on in his life that we know nothing about," Brian allowed. "After all, there's more to life than work, and we all have skeletons in our closet. Things we'd rather other people didn't know about. Maybe he was having personal issues. Woman trouble. Or money. Debt. That sort of thing."

"Well, I'm sure the authorities will get to the bottom of it," said Paula. "We just wanted to let you know what happened."

"Thanks. I appreciate it." His voice seemed distracted, as if his mind was already elsewhere, mulling over what he'd just been told.

"We'll let you go now, Brian. Take care of yourself."

"Ah, yes, of course. Right. Will do. And do keep me informed of developments, will you?"

Paula pressed the button to end the call. "What do you make of that?"

"Interesting. I suppose we'll have to wait and see what the police have to say, but I thought the same about Edmund as Brian did. He was enthusiastic. Had an energy about him in rehearsals that the cast seemed to be picking up on.

And speaking of the cast, they'll have seen the police tape around his bungalow and wonder what's going on. The grapevine will be going wild. Someone's got to let everyone in the company know what's happened."

"Well, that would be you. Who else is there? As I said earlier, you're the most senior staff member, the one everybody knows and trusts."

"In that case, then, let's ask Wade to join us. He can talk about the production. We'll need to get onto him right away so he can prepare. I'll ask Aaron to call an emergency meeting of the cast and crew. Let's say four o'clock this afternoon in the theater. And we should see if Ray's available to answer questions and reassure them. Maybe he'll even be able to give us an update."

Chapter 13

Just before four, the cast and crew of the Catskills Shakespeare Theater Company filed into the theater and took their seats. There was no good-natured chatter or jostling; they just moved quietly, filling the rows. Audrey had taken a seat in the front row, and Mattie sat in an aisle seat in the second row. Everyone remained silent, respectful, and expectant. Four chairs had been arranged on the stage.

At four o'clock on the dot, Charlotte led Ray, Paula Van Dusen, and Wade Radcliffe onstage. They'd had a brief chat a few minutes earlier and had settled on a speaking order. Ray, Paula, and Wade sat as Charlotte took her place at the edge of the stage.

"Thank you for coming," she began. "There's no way to sugarcoat this, so I'm just going to get right to it. You probably saw a lot of police activity here today, and I'm sure you've heard some rumors. So I'm sorry to have to tell you that our director, Edmund Albright, was found dead in his bungalow this morning." She paused, but the gasps of surprise and dismay she had expected did not come. At that moment, the back door of the theater opened and local reporter Fletcher Macmillan scuttled down the aisle. He slid into a seat behind the cast and crew members and nodded at Charlotte to continue. Incensed that he was here at all, had arrived late, and then in effect had given her permission to continue speaking at her own meeting, she took a calming breath and continued.

"The police are investigating the cause of death, and that's why our local police chief, Ray Nicholson, is here. He's also here because he's a member of our community. You all know Ray. He sometimes works our prompt desk during performances, and he lives here in the grounds of the hotel with, well, me." Ray took his place beside her, and she looked at him gratefully and touched his arm. "Ray," she said simply and stepped back and took a seat beside Paula.

"We answered a call midmorning that a deceased person with a gunshot wound had been found in the director's bungalow," he said. "The Criminal Investigation Bureau of the state police were called in, and they've taken over the investigation. Although the body hasn't been formally identified, we are confident it is that of Edmund Albright. Cause of death hasn't been determined, and at this point, we aren't prepared to discuss the circumstances under which he died." In response, the crowd murmured and a hand shot up.

"What's your best guess?" a young actor asked.

"Sorry, not going to speculate about that," Ray replied. "But we should know more soon, and when we do, the details will be released through the appropriate channels. When we know, you'll know." Charlotte's eyes wandered over the group and came to rest on Fletcher Macmillan. She had no idea who had informed him of the meeting but now realized it might be good that he was here. He could get all his questions answered, and they'd only have to go through this once. Fletcher scribbled down Ray's response and then looked up from his notebook, waiting for the next newsworthy item. He was saving his questions for the end.

"But do you think any of us are in any danger?" asked an elderly actress.

"No," said Ray. "There's no reason to think that. But of course you should observe all the usual precautions. Be careful walking alone at night and make sure your doors are locked." He scanned the group, his eyes coming to rest on Fletcher Macmillan. "Any other questions?"

When no one responded, he gave a little nod and then sat beside Charlotte as Paula stood up and took her place at the front of the stage. She introduced herself as the theater's board chair and then discussed the major issue facing the company.

"And because it's vitally important to the viability of the company that the show does go on, Wade Radcliffe has agreed to step in as our new director. I know this is not an ideal situation for you. He's the third director to work on this project, and that brings all kinds of creative and logistical problems, but I have to ask you to work with him. You're all professionals, and I know that you'll do what it takes to get *Much Ado About Nothing* up and running. Oh, and by the way, I spoke to Brian Prentice earlier this afternoon. He's doing well and sends his best regards to everybody." A smatter of light applause broke out at the mention of their former colleague's name. "Right, well, let me introduce you to your new director, Wade Radcliffe." She listed his accomplishments and then, after inviting him to speak to the cast and crew he'd be working with, extended a welcoming hand in his direction.

Wade strolled toward the edge of the stage, folded his arms, and took a moment to make eye contact with the audience before speaking.

"I'm sorry we have to get to know one another under these unfortunate circumstances," he began. His voice easily filled the theater, and his words revealed a trace of a Boston accent. "But this is the way it is. None of us wants to see this theater—or any other theater, for that matter—dark. So we have to find a way to work together to get this play ready for opening night. Opening night can't be postponed. It's going to take long hours of rehearsals. Some scenes, like the aborted wedding between Hero and Claudio, are going to require more time than others. I hope you're all well rested and have your lines down, because we start tomorrow. I'll post a schedule this evening. There won't be time for prima donna behavior. We're not going to worry too much about blocking at this point. It should become obvious during rehearsals who's going to stand where. I'm asking you to give me your best from the beginning. All of us have to work together to make this happen."

He paused for a moment, and when a hand went up, he continued. "I haven't finished speaking yet. When I'm done, I'll take questions, and anyway, I think I know what you were just about to ask. I'm coming to that. The board of directors has decreed that we must continue with the Civil War theme. I'm not in favor of it, I'll tell you that right now, but those are our instructions, and we must make the best of it."

From her onstage viewpoint, facing the audience, Charlotte could see their facial expressions change from a neutral blankness to puzzlement to open surprise. A couple of mouths in the front row were shaped into round little *Os*. Beside her, Paula Van Dusen stiffened, then shielded her eyes from the lights to see the audience better.

"And now's the time for questions," Wade Radcliffe announced. "Anybody?"

Audrey raised her hand, and Wade acknowledged her.

"Will you be making any casting changes?" Off to her left, Mattie Lane perked up.

"No. We don't have time for you to learn new lines."

Frowning, Mattie sank back into her seat and whispered something to the actor sitting beside her. He gave a little shrug, and Mattie turned her attention back to the stage.

"Well, if there's nothing else, let's leave it there for now," said Wade. "I'm looking forward to working with you and putting on the best version possible of this great play."

Fletcher Macmillan stood up. "Did you have a chance to talk to the previous director about the Civil War theme, Wade?" he asked.

"No, I didn't."

"How do you feel about getting this job under these circumstances?"

"My pleasure at being here is tempered by my regret and sadness that I was offered this opportunity because of the unfortunate death of a young director who was showing signs of great promise. A great loss to the theater."

"Tempered by regret and sadness?" That sounds like the carefully crafted rubbish a public relations person would write, thought Charlotte. *Wade certainly didn't come up with that off the top of his head.* Macmillan scribbled it all down and then flipped the page of his notebook.

"If there are no more questions, we'll leave it there for now," Wade repeated. "And I'll see everyone bright and early tomorrow, ready to go, in the rehearsal room. Remember, check the schedule this evening so you don't miss your call."

Macmillan waved his notebook. "Just one more question. For the police chief. Has the deceased's family been notified?"

"Yes," said Ray, getting to his feet. "They have."

As the company began to file out, Wade faced Ray, Charlotte, and Paula.

"Well, I think that went well, don't you?" he asked, removing his glasses and wiping the lenses on his shirt.

Paula turned to Ray and Charlotte. "I'm going to need a moment alone with Mr. Radcliffe," she said. "If you wouldn't mind, I'll meet you at your bungalow in a few minutes."

Ray took Charlotte's hand, and the two of them disappeared behind the curtains and offstage. When Charlotte slowed, Ray pulled her forward. "No you don't," he said. "No listening. Come on. We're leaving."

When the auditorium was empty, Paula turned to Wade. "This will just take a minute, and then you can be on your way. You have a rehearsal schedule to prepare, I believe. Now then. How do I think this meeting with the cast and crew went? It could have gone better. You could have done more to reassure them and get them on side. I don't think you made too many friends. And in the future, please don't speak of the board of this theatrical company in such disparaging terms. It was very wrong of you to tell the cast that you disagreed with the board's decision about the Civil War theme."

Radcliffe opened his mouth to speak but couldn't shape the words and closed it again.

"Now, look, Wade," Paula continued with a softening of her previously imperious tone, "you've been given this opportunity under difficult circumstances, and we appreciate your stepping in like this to help us out. But we really need this relationship to work. So let's just put this behind us and move on. And let's all get on the same page. Maybe you could bring a little enthusiasm to the first rehearsal so everyone picks up on that from you. And you know, we weren't so keen on the Civil War idea at first, either, but it kind of grows on you." She gave him an encouraging smile and touched his upper arm. "Think about it and give it a chance."

"Could I just say something?"

"Of course."

"I'm truly sorry about Albright. He was young. A great shame. And when he died, I thought you might ask me to step in and help out, and I was happy to be given this opportunity. But I didn't think for one minute that I would be asked to put on his vision of the play. It's incredibly difficult for a director to pick up someone else's thoughts and make it happen. You have to believe in what you're doing, and frankly, I'm not sure that I do. But you know how much this job means to me, and how much I wanted it, so I'll gladly do whatever I'm asked to do."

*

"Well, what did you think?" asked Ray as he held the back door of the hotel open for Charlotte.

"It's hard to tell, isn't it? Most of them are actors, so they can hide their true feelings a little better than the rest of us. They seemed shocked when Wade told them he didn't like the Civil War idea but that he was prepared to hold his nose and get on with it."

"Or words to that effect."

"Paula obviously wasn't pleased with Wade's remarks. I expect she's taking him to task now." Ray unlocked the bungalow and Charlotte leaned over to greet Rupert. "I'm going to walk Rupert back to the hotel to meet Paula. She'll be more than ready for a G&T, so why don't you sort out the drinks?"

Paula and Wade were emerging from the hotel just as Rupert and Charlotte reached the graveled parking area. Wade and Paula exchanged a handshake, and then, with a vague wave in Charlotte's direction, Wade headed for his car. Paula reached Charlotte, gave Rupert a pat, and straightened up.

"Well?" said Charlotte.

She let out a little moan of exasperation. "What's that English expression you have? 'I could murder a drink.' Well, I could."

"Ray's fixing it for you right now."

When they reached the bungalow, Charlotte unclipped Rupert's leash, and the three made their way around to the front of the structure where Ray was waiting. He held out a frosty glass with a napkin wrapped around the base to Paula.

When they were seated, Paula took an appreciative sip and then addressed Ray.

"There is something we need to talk about, and that's the director's bungalow. Fortunately, we don't need it just now because Wade lives locally, but at some point, it'll need to be cleaned and made habitable. How long before the police turn it over to us?"

"A few more days. The body's been removed, but they'll do more tests."

"I expect Harvey will have to hire one of those companies that specialize in, ah, delicate cleaning jobs," said Charlotte. "There will be . . . what do they call it?"

"Biohazardous material," Ray answered.

"And I guess there will be a lot of formality and legality around his death," said Paula.

"There's a lot of legality around any death," said Ray.

"What I meant was, will a family member have to come from England to identify the body?"

"Audrey might be able to do that. She knew him previously. And then all his effects will have to be packaged for return to his next of kin or estate."

"Are the police any closer to determining if it was suicide?" Charlotte asked.

"Autopsy in the morning should help with that," he replied. Paula and Charlotte exchanged a quick glance that Ray picked up on. "What?"

"We don't think he committed suicide," said Charlotte. "He was too excited and happy to be here. Was there a note?"

"No," said Ray. "But that doesn't necessarily mean anything. People don't always leave a note."

When Paula had gone, Charlotte looked at the empty glass she'd set down on the table and sighed.

"She lives so elegantly, Paula does. Lunch today was so lovely. Delicious food, beautiful surroundings, fresh flowers from her own gardens. Everything was just perfect. I wonder sometimes what she thinks when she comes here. How shabby it must all seem. And now, with Edmund's death, rather sordid."

Chapter 14

The nights were drawing in, and it was dark by the time Charlotte and Ray returned from dinner at the Thai restaurant.

With the lights of the hotel behind them and in the semirural setting, the sky on this clear, cool night was visible in a way most city dwellers never get to see. A firmament, filled with an infinite number of glittering stars against a sea of black velvet, twinkled above them, and a waning crescent moon hung low in the sky. Soft, ambient sounds, broken only by the swish of an occasional vehicle on the nearby two-lane highway, enveloped them. Wrapped up in each other, hand in hand, their bodies close together, they walked down the little path that led to Charlotte's bungalow. She still thought of it as "her bungalow" and referred to it as "her bungalow," but it increasingly felt like "their bungalow."

Charlotte unlocked the door, greeted Rupert, and clipped on his leash. She handed this to Ray, who walked off into the night with him. Charlotte closed the door behind them, put the food she'd brought home in the fridge, and set out two brandy snifters. She poured two small drinks and took them through to the sitting room to await his return.

*

The ringing of his phone jolted Ray awake. His adrenalin pumping as he picked it up off the nightstand, he gently pulled the covers back and eased out of bed, trying not to wake Charlotte.

"What is it, Phil?" he whispered into his phone as he slipped into the hallway. He listened for a moment, then returned to the bedroom. As an on-call police officer, he always left his uniform where he could find it in a hurry, in the dark.

Charlotte stirred as he gathered up his clothing.

"What time is it?" she asked, her voice hoarse with sleep. "What's happening? Are you going out?"

"Yeah, sorry. Got a callout," he said. "I tried not to wake you."

"But you're not on call tonight," she protested. "Why do you have to go? Why can't Phil go?"

"The caller asked for me," he said, "and I'm closer."

Clutching the bedclothes to her chest, Charlotte, now wide awake, sat up, switched on the lamp, and checked the time on her bedside clock.

"Ray! What's happening? It's two o'clock."

He leaned over and kissed her. "We got a call that there might be a prowler in the hotel grounds. It's probably nothing, but I've got to check it out. I'll be back as soon as I can. Try to go back to sleep."

"Who phoned?" Ray didn't answer as he finished buttoning his shirt. Charlotte repeated the question and then answered it herself. "It was Audrey, wasn't it?"

Ray grunted an affirmative as he put on his boots.

"Where's Rupert?" Charlotte asked. "I want him with me."

Ray lifted him onto the bed. "Here he is. I've got to go. I'll lock the door behind me. Don't open it to anyone except me or Phil."

*

Ray raced to his car, grabbed a flashlight, and headed back toward the three bungalows. The moon was now obscured by heavy cloud cover, making it difficult to see beyond the beam of the flashlight. He reached Charlotte's bungalow, paused to shine his flashlight in the shrubbery around it, and then hurried on to the director's bungalow, again pointing the beam in the overgrown bushes that threatened to overwhelm the structure. Pausing for a moment to listen and hearing nothing, he continued on to the star bungalow. He circled it, again shining his flashlight in the bushes, and when he was satisfied no one was hiding in them, he knocked on the door.

"Police," he called out. The door was cautiously opened, and Audrey Ashley collapsed in his arms. He steadied her, then led her into the sitting room and lowered her gently into the center of the sofa. She shifted down to the end so she was bathed in the soft, warm glow of the one lamp in the room that had been switched on. She was wearing a knee-length mint-green nightgown and matching jacket. Ray picked up the decorative blanket draped over the arm of the sofa and, standing above her, placed it casually around her shoulders. She pulled the blanket tightly around her and clutched it in front of her chest with both hands as Ray eased himself into a nearby chair. He shifted the chair back an inch or two, so he was in shadow, outside the small circle of lamplight.

"I had a good look around your bungalow and the one next door, and there's no sign of anyone. Whoever it was, he's gone. Now can you just tell me what happened here tonight?" He flipped open a notebook and waited for her response.

"I was going over the script for tomorrow in bed," she said, "reading lines and repeating them back to myself, when I heard someone rustling about outside my bedroom window. I didn't know what to do, so I called the police."

"It's late to be up reading," Ray commented.

"I had a little nap after dinner, so I had trouble getting to sleep," she said. "Maybe it's a result of years of performing at night, but my sleeping patterns are out of whack. I wake up early and either take an afternoon nap or go to bed early, and then I'm wide awake at the most inconvenient times."

"So you were reading and your light was on. Were the blinds open or closed?"

"There isn't a blind, just a curtain. And it was half-way open, I guess." Ray stood up and disappeared into the bedroom.

"Did you turn the light off and look out the window?" he continued when he returned. "Did you actually see anyone?" She lowered her chin, shook her head slightly, and peered up at him through long, thick eyelashes.

"I feel so vulnerable here. Anyone can wander into the grounds, and there's no security. I'm so glad you were able to come, but I can't call you every night, can I?" She laughed lightly.

"We'd rather be called out, just to be on the safe side, than have something bad happen. And your sister. Is she here?"

"I didn't wake her. She can sleep through anything."

Ray asked a few more questions for his report and then wrapped up the interview. "It's almost three o'clock. I'll be off now and let you get back to sleep."

"Oh, but I don't know if I'd be able to sleep! Couldn't you just stay here a little longer?"

"Whoever it was is gone, and you'll be quite safe now. The windows are new, and the locks are secure. But if you'd be more comfortable, I could see if rooms can be arranged for you and your sister in the hotel for the rest of the night."

"Oh, I don't think so. One doesn't like to make a fuss, and it'll be morning soon enough."

"Well, I'm going to recommend again that the bushes around all the bungalows be trimmed right back. This probably could have been avoided if Harvey had done that the first time I asked." He gazed around the room, taking in the fresh decor. "Looks very nice." Ray moved toward the door and said goodnight. A few minutes later, he unlocked the door to Charlotte's bungalow.

"I don't think there was a prowler at all," he said as he undressed. "Something about it just didn't ring true."

"Well, she is an actress. You'd think she could have been a little more convincing."

Ray pulled back the covers and slid in beside Charlotte, taking her in his arms. "She was wearing makeup, and lots of it," he said into the back of her neck.

"Ah," said Charlotte. "I get it. She would have cleansed and moisturized her face before going to bed."

"So if you thought you there was a prowler in the shrubbery under your window, would you take the time to put on makeup? And I'm not talking about just a bit of lipstick. Her face was covered in it. What's that stuff called?"

"Foundation."

"And the color on the eyes. I don't know how long it takes to put on that much makeup, and maybe because she's an actress she can do it quickly, but I think she had it all in place before she called the police."

"She wanted to look her best for you."

Ray closed his eyes. "Her bungalow looked really nice. You and Paula did a great job," he murmured. "Flowers everywhere."

Charlotte's eyes flew open.

Chapter 15

On Wednesday, just before lunch, the police tape barricading the director's bungalow was taken down. Charlotte called Nancy to let her know the state police were finished with the building and volunteered to gather up Edmund Albright's personal effects. Nancy, in the midst of budget preparations, had welcomed the suggestion. And so, avoiding the indignity of green garbage bags and assuming the luggage he'd arrived with would still be there, Charlotte arrived with just a banker's box. She unlocked the bungalow with the key Nancy had sent over and entered the still, empty kitchen.

The teapot remained on the table where she had last seen it, beside a little pile of papers. Since the police forensics team had finished their work here and turned the property over to its owner, there was no reason she couldn't touch anything she wanted to. So she picked up the teapot and was about to empty its contents when something stopped her. She took out her phone and snapped a photograph of the two floating tea bags before pouring the stale tea down the sink, rinsing the pot, and placing it the cupboard.

Turning her attention to the papers on the table, she set aside the blocking notes the first director, Simon Dyer, had left behind and concentrated on the documents written by Edmund Albright. One was a list of every prop needed in the play, and a second document, attached to it, showed where he wanted every item placed on the props table and how he wanted it labeled. She placed Edmund's papers in the banker's box and turned her attention to the sitting room. She hadn't actually entered the room on the morning she discovered the body, but now she'd have to walk through it, and past the sofa, to reach the bedroom.

She steeled herself and entered the sitting room. The room had a faintly chemical smell that she guessed came from the materials the police had used in their forensic analysis. The odor was slightly sharp, but not unpleasant. Specks of dried blood remained on the wall and sofa cushions. The closed curtains gave the room a depressing air, so she pulled them open and was slightly uplifted by the sight of the trees that surrounded the bungalow, swaying lightly in the breeze, their living, waving branches casting a moving pattern on the faded carpet.

She entered the bedroom. The closet door was open, presumably left that way by police investigators, revealing a large black suitcase, familiar to anyone who has ever waited at an airport luggage carousel. She tugged it out of the closet, lifted it onto the bed, unzipped the lid, and flung it open. She emptied the drawers, and after folding all the clothing, she placed it neatly in the suitcase. She returned to the closet, removed the shirts and trousers from the hangers, and set them on the bed, then cleared all the toiletries out of the bathroom.

She went through the pockets of the garments one by one, placing each item of clothing in the case, and when it was full, she checked the clothes closet one last time and then zipped the suitcase shut and pulled it behind her through to the kitchen, its little wheels clacking on the tile floor the only sound she'd heard since she entered the bungalow. She opened the door to the small cupboard beside the door and found, hanging on a hook, the beige jacket Edmund had carried on his arrival and worn at rehearsals. She lifted it out, checked the pockets, and set the contents on the kitchen table. A used tissue and a receipt from Bentley's Bistro. She examined the receipt. Two coffees and one chocolate croissant. She folded the jacket, zippered it into the suitcase's side pocket, and after a moment's hesitation, held onto the receipt.

With a final look around the kitchen, she switched off the light, locked the door, and walked home.

Chapter 16

Charlotte unlocked the door to her bungalow and went in search of Rupert, who was lying on her bed, sound asleep. She lay down beside him and stroked his soft fur.

"What do you think happened in that bungalow, Rupert?" He looked at her with adoring brown eyes and then, at the sound of someone knocking on the door, jumped off the bed and ran to the door.

He gave a couple of short, sharp barks and then looked at Charlotte to make sure she understood something needed to be done.

"Who is it, Rupert?"

She opened the door to find Aaron on the steps.

"This arrived," he said, holding out a letter. "It's from England, and Nancy thought you'd be the best person to deal with it, so she asked me to give it to you. I should have given it to you yesterday, but things got busy, and I'm sorry I forgot. Anyway, here it is. Nancy thought you might want to show it to Ray and let them deal with it."

After thanking Aaron, Charlotte withdrew the letter from the envelope that had been neatly sliced open and read it twice.

*

Early mornings were now cooler, with a mysterious mist that wreathed the mountaintops and skimmed along the surface of the river. But by midmorning, chased away by the Catskills sun, the mist disappeared, leaving behind crisp, clean air filled with the promise of the autumn soon to come. And now, at lunchtime, the temperature was comfortably warm. Charlotte loved this time of year. The worst of the summer heat was behind them, and the short days filled with wind and rain that would lead into winter were yet to come. This was a day to be enjoyed.

With Rupert scampering ahead, they walked along the path that led to the wooded area at the end of the hotel property. As they reached the star bungalow, the door opened, and Maxine emerged. Charlotte and Rupert slowed their pace, and Maxine joined them.

"Hello," said Charlotte. "Are you finding enough to keep you busy while Audrey's in rehearsal?"

"Oh, yes. I'm well used to this. Once the play is running, I'll be so busy looking after her. And you must let me know what I can do to help you too, if I can."

"Oh, that's very kind," said Charlotte. "We're so short staffed, your help would be very welcome. Especially as you know your way around a theater."

"Yes, we all grew up in the theater, but we soon recognized that Audrey was the one with the talent, so we put all the family resources into supporting her." She gestured at Rupert. "I've seen you walking past with your dog. Mine's had to stay with a friend until I get home. He's a Jack Russell, and I can't tell you how much I miss him. Walking without a dog always seems so pointless. Do you mind if I walk with you?"

"Not at all. I can certainly appreciate how much you must miss your dog. Rupert and I have never really been apart. And as for being here, settling in all right, are you?"

"Oh, yes. I like the small-town atmosphere. Audrey's more for the big city. She loves London and New York, but I'm very happy here. I walk into town and pop into the shops, and it's all very interesting. I feel right at home, in many ways."

"Tell me, did you know Edmund Albright in England at all?"

"Oh, yes, our paths crossed a few times."

"What did you think of him?"

"I think he had an overinflated sense of his own importance. Full of himself, really. In my opinion, he thought of himself as a highflyer, but he couldn't quite find his wings. He really wasn't all that, if you know what I mean. But he was more than confident in his own abilities, and sometimes that fooled people into thinking he was better than he was."

"Interesting. And Audrey had worked with him before, of course."

"He was the assistant director on a play she did in Manchester. She liked him. Thought he had a talent for getting the best out of the actors. Out here, though, she saw a different side of him, and she didn't like it. She regretted exercising her director approval to bring him here, although he was thrilled to be asked and couldn't get here fast enough."

"Yes, so I gathered."

Interesting smells led Rupert scurrying into the undergrowth, and the women walked on without him.

"And that ridiculous Civil War idea of his. Positively daft! What did he hope to accomplish with that? Call me old fashioned, but I don't see the point of messing about with good old Elizabethan and Jacobean productions. Everything else is just a gimmick. So unnecessary."

"You and Wade Radcliffe seem to be on the same page with that. And it's causing endless problems in the costume department, I can tell you."

"I wanted to talk to you about that, actually. It's critically important that Audrey look fabulous in the publicity photographs, so you will come up with some becoming costumes, won't you?"

"Yes," Charlotte promised, "I certainly will."

They had reached the turning around point at the end of the property, where Rupert caught up and assumed his place in front of them for the return journey.

"Tell me, Maxine," Charlotte said, "do you think Edmund capable of killing himself?"

Maxine took her time before replying. "I think anyone is capable of just about anything, in the right circumstances." She stopped to pick up a leaf and examine it. "Why? Have the police said for sure it was suicide?"

"Not that I've heard, but as far as I know, that seems to be the theory they're working on."

They had reached the star bungalow and stopped. "I was going to walk into town, so I think I'll just fetch a jacket," said Maxine. "It can get a little chilly on the way home, once the sun isn't so directly overhead anymore." A vase filled with roses in the window caught Charlotte's eye.

"Oh, those flowers," Maxine said, following Charlotte's gaze. "Somebody keeps sending them. We wake up in the morning, and there they are. We don't know who, but Audrey's had admirers almost her whole life."

"They look lovely. Well, bye for now. We'll talk soon, I'm sure."

Maxine disappeared into her bungalow, and Charlotte and Rupert returned home.

She opened the door to find Ray seated at the kitchen table, eating a cheese-and-tomato sandwich.

"Oh, there you are," he said. "I thought you and Rupert would be back soon. I made a sandwich for you too. It's in the fridge." She took it out, cut it in four, and took it to the table.

"Got some news," Ray said when she was seated. "With the forensics from the bungalow and the autopsy results, the medical examiner is fairly certain that the death of Edmund

Albright was a suicide. Still some test results to come in, though, so it's not been officially decided yet. It's 'pending.'"

"Fairly certain?" Charlotte's eyes widened. "Really?"

"The forensics include blood spatter, gunshot residue, angle of entry . . . everything."

"Does it, though?" asked Charlotte. "Does it really include everything?"

"What do you mean?"

"Well, where did he get the gun? Where is there a record of him buying a gun? Or registering it?"

"He didn't have to buy it. It was already there. And by 'there,' I mean probably right in his bungalow."

"What do you mean?"

"The gun was registered to Simon Dyer."

Charlotte gasped. "Simon! You mean Simon left a gun behind when he moved back to Colorado?"

"Apparently."

"But why would he leave a gun behind?"

Ray took a sip of soda. "My guess is that the gun was just too much trouble. New York State has strict gun laws. If he wanted to move out of state with the gun, he was required to notify the office where he registered the gun. You say he left in a hurry, so he probably didn't have time for that. If he was flying, well, a handgun has to be checked baggage in a locked, hard-sided container. If he was driving, the laws about guns vary from state to state, so bringing it with him would have been a nightmare. And I have no idea about gun laws in Colorado, so the way I see it, it was just easier for Simon to leave the gun behind. It was way more trouble than it was worth."

"Where did he leave it?"

"We don't know, but it's possible he stashed it somewhere in the bungalow. He might have tried to hide it, hoping it would never be found."

Charlotte gave a little shrug of mild disagreement. "I looked around his bungalow after he left, and I didn't see a gun."

"Well, you were just having a casual look around, weren't you? If you'd been living in the place, like Edmund was, you'd have been into all the drawers and cupboards, and you might have found it. I doubt you looked in all the places where a gun might be kept or hidden, but Edmund probably just opened a drawer or a cupboard and reached behind something, and there it was. But the investigators will talk to Simon and find out the details about the gun. They'll get to the bottom of it."

"All right. So let's say Simon did leave the gun behind—along with ammunition, of course—and Edmund found it. Why do the police think his death was a suicide? How do they know it wasn't accidental?"

"Doubtful. People don't usually shoot themselves accidentally in the head."

"Maybe not, but police do get suicides wrong. How many times have you seen stories on the television where the police determine someone committed suicide and other experts say that's impossible? That the victim would have had to have arms eight feet long to pull the trigger at that angle, but someone else—the murderer, let's say—could have it done quite easily?"

"I suppose that happens occasionally."

"I think the police got it wrong this time."

"Do you base that on anything, or is it just a hunch?"

"Well, first of all, guns are such an American thing. Edmund was English. If Edmund had wanted to commit suicide, which I don't think he did, I don't think he'd have shot himself. That's just not what an English person would do.

"And there's something else bothering me," said Charlotte. "Did the police process the bungalow properly? Or did they just go in there assuming it was a suicide and then look for things to confirm their theory so they could get everything wrapped up quickly?"

"What are you getting at?"

"There was a teapot on the table. Still had a bit of tea left in it. But there were no teacups. It looked to me as if someone had been in that bungalow drinking tea with Edmund shortly before he died. And quite possibly, that person killed him."

"Wow, that's a big leap to make from a teapot."

"It is, but you see, Ray, there were two tea bags in the pot. Now an English person making tea just for himself would use one tea bag, not two. And, God forbid, he might even just make the tea in a cup and not even bother with the teapot. And here's something else: If

Edmund was alone, washed his teacup, and put it away, why wouldn't he empty the teapot and rinse it out at the same time? That's just how you do it. You've seen me do that a hundred times."

Ray's eyes narrowed slightly. "Go on."

"I think someone else was with him in the bungalow on the night he died, drinking tea in the sitting room, and before they left, the other person remembered to rinse out the teacups and put them away, but maybe they were in a hurry and forgot about the teapot sitting on the kitchen table. I think your police colleagues should take a closer look at this case to be absolutely certain that it really was Edmund Albright who pulled that trigger."

"Charlotte," Ray said gently, "they've conducted their investigation, and the evidence has led them to the conclusion that suicide is likely."

"Well, I think it's highly unlikely. I think they're wrong. Is there any evidence that Edmund Albright was in the right frame of mind to commit suicide? That he was depressed or unhappy? That he was overcome by financial or emotional problems he felt he couldn't solve?"

Ray shook his head. "I haven't heard anything like that."

"Exactly. Quite the opposite. Everyone thought he was happy to be in America and that he was really excited about working on the play.

"And here's one more last bit of information to back up my theory." Ray raised an eyebrow.

She dropped the letter Aaron had delivered on the table.

"His desperate mother, not knowing who to turn to, wrote to the theater company asking for help. She doesn't believe he would have taken his own life, either, and wants to know how to get the police to investigate a cause of death other than suicide. Don't you think the police owe it to her to just consider the possibility that Edmund's death wasn't suicide? Shouldn't they look at all possibilities?"

She wiped her hands on her paper napkin, crumpled it, and dropped it on her plate. Certain that Edmund's death was neither accidental nor suicide, she shot Ray a determined look filled with meaningful purpose.

"Oh, oh," he said. "I know that look."

She smiled sweetly at him. "Well, it's too bad you're not seeing the same look around that police station of yours, because it's the look of someone who's not going to let somebody get away with murder."

Chapter 17

In the hotel's heyday, the large room down the hall from what was now the theater auditorium had been the day care center. Back then, parents eager for a day of tennis, swimming, and lounging by the pool with cocktails dropped off their precious offspring after breakfast and picked them up before dinner. Now the room—with its green-tiled floor, red plastic chairs stacked or set around the room, bicycle leaning against one wall, and a couple of old tables upon which actors had placed scripts, bottles of water, and coffee cups—was the theater company's rehearsal space.

"Could I ask you to gather 'round, please?" Wade Radcliffe clapped his hands, and the low level of chatter died away. "Just like in Shakespeare's day, when there was barely any rehearsal time, we don't have the luxury of a lot of time to prepare for this production. And that's unfortunate because there's so much we could explore, so much subtext to discuss.

"However, I worked on the text overnight, and I've also researched the RSC production that was set after World War I in an English country house. So like many of you, I've come around to the idea of setting this play after the Civil War. I now think it's an intriguing idea that will make for a dynamic American theater experience."

The cast members smiled at one another, and the heaviness that had been weighing on the company began to dissipate.

"Now *Much Ado* is grouped in with the comedies, and people tend to think of it as frothy, but I think it's a dark play, with some comic scenes scattered throughout." Several cast members nodded in agreement, and a couple took a few steps closer to him. Charlotte, with Aaron seated beside her at a table with their backs to the wall so they could observe the rehearsal, took that as an encouraging sign.

"Now the military side of things is going to be much more pronounced because we're setting our version right after the Civil War. And the war could explain a lot of the characters' somewhat erratic behavior." He looked at Charlotte. "Now let's talk about act one, scene one, when we first meet the soldiers. I liked the idea of Don Pedro fighting for the North and Don John for the South. That would instantly explain their estrangement to the audience. They'd understand immediately." Charlotte made a note. One men's gray Southern uniform costume. The rest would be the Union blue of the North.

Beside her, Aaron listened carefully. She was glad she'd agreed to his request to design and create the women's costumes, leaving her to arrange the rental of the men's costumes.

"I don't see Mattie," Charlotte remarked in a low voice, leaning over to him. "Have you spoken to her in the last day or two?"

Aaron shook his head. "But I've got her measurements on file. I can go ahead with her dress." He tucked his pencil behind his ear and tilted his sketch pad toward Charlotte. "What do you think?" Charlotte peered at the gray-and-white outline.

"Who is this for? Before you show a costume sketch to anyone, and that includes me, write the name of the character on it. Otherwise, how am I supposed to know if it's appropriate or not? Is this for Hero?"

"No, it's for Beatrice."

"Could be too fancy. We'll talk about it outside, later. Don't want to talk while Wade is speaking to the cast. It's rude, and besides, we might miss something important."

The bar that opened the door lowered, signaling someone was pressing on it from the corridor. A moment later, the door opened slowly, and Mattie crept in. She aimed an apologetic look in the direction of Wade Radcliffe, but he did not stop speaking and he did not acknowledge her arrival. Arriving late for rehearsal is a cardinal sin in the acting world; it disrupts the work in progress, can cause delays, and is considered highly unprofessional. It can even cause an actor to lose a part.

Dressed in a green-and-white-striped shirt tucked neatly into his jeans, Wade continued working with the actors, inviting them to explain how they saw their characters' interactions with others. Charlotte frowned as Mattie hovered on the fringe of the group; her participation level was low, and what there was of it seemed desultory and forced. Finally, the director called a break. The actor playing Claudio, Hero's love interest who cruelly rejects her at the altar after believing malicious lies about her, approached Mattie and rested his hand on her arm as he spoke to her. She shook her head and turned away.

"Something's not right with Mattie," Charlotte said to Aaron. He looked up from his sketching.

"She can be a bit moody. Best thing is to leave her alone when she's like that. She's probably having an off day."

"Maybe. I'm going for a coffee now, but I'll try to have a word with Mattie later to make sure she's okay. You coming?"

Aaron tucked his pencil behind his ear and shuffled his sketches into some sort of order. "I guess so." As they walked down the corridor to the cafeteria with the rest of the company, Aaron asked, "What did you want to tell me about the sketch? You said it might be too fancy."

"Have you read the play?"

"Well, not all of it. I find the language pretty heavy going."

"Yes, well, the thing is, Beatrice is Leonato's niece, which makes her Hero's cousin. She's the poor relation, really, and may have some responsibilities running the household.

Remember what I told you about how we use costumes to reflect status and social importance? To show a character's place in the hierarchy? So Beatrice can't be dressed to the same standards as Hero, who is wealthier. So here you have the servants' clothes." She made a gesture with the palm of her hand facing down and then raised her hand. "And here you have Beatrice." She raised her hand again. "And at the top, in terms of women's dress, you have Hero.

"So if Beatrice is wearing a simple calico dress, then you can add some finery to Hero's to indicate she is wealthier. Bits of lace, maybe. Or her dress is made from a more expensive fabric. But remember, there's been a war on, so their costumes should reflect that. Maybe their dresses are faded and worn because they haven't been able to buy new material. Think it through. But whatever you do, Beatrice's dress has to be flattering to Audrey. So you've got your work cut out for you."

"Not yet I haven't," Aaron replied, and they both grinned.

The cafeteria was crowded and noisy with collegial banter. Wade Radcliffe had chosen a seat in the middle of a long table, where several actors had joined him. Seated beside him, and beaming up at him with everything she had, was Audrey Ashley. He smiled at her and then looked around the room. *He's in his element*, thought Charlotte. *He's doing what he loves, and he belongs here.*

Spotting Mattie hesitating in the doorway, Charlotte waved her over. "Would you like Aaron to get you a cup of coffee?"

"Yeah, that would be great, thanks."

When he was out of earshot, Charlotte turned to Mattie. "I'm worried about you. You were late this morning. That's not like you. And when you were here, you seemed distracted and not at all your usual self. Is everything all right?"

Mattie looked at her hands resting in her lap.

"No," she said. "I don't think it is. I wasn't just late for rehearsal. I'm . . . late, as in, you know. Late." She gave Charlotte a beseeching look. "Late."

The background noise in the cafeteria disappeared as Charlotte focused intently on what Mattie was saying. She touched Mattie's hand. "How late?"

Mattie let out a long, slow breath. "I've been a bit worried for a few days."

Aaron returned and set a takeaway cup of coffee in front of her. "I got it to go," he said, "because Wade wants everyone back to the rehearsal in a few minutes."

Mattie nodded her thanks but didn't meet his eyes and didn't touch the coffee. Charlotte picked it up and took it with them.

Chapter 18

With the cast enthused and energized, Wade led everyone back to the rehearsal room. Several younger actors clustered around him, gesturing with their hands as they asked questions or suggested motivations for their characters. They had just reached the rehearsal room when Charlotte's phone alerted her to a text.

"Harvey wants me to come to the front desk," she said to Aaron. "You carry on and pay attention to what Wade says, but I think we've got all the information we need to get started."

When she started working with this theater company, it had taken her ages to find her way through the labyrinth of hallways that led from the backstage theater area to the hotel's front desk without getting hopelessly lost, but now she navigated her way easily and efficiently, taking the shortest route, until she reached the door that opened onto the lobby. Harvey's head turned toward the sound of the opening door. He stood behind the reception desk, arms folded, in front of a large spray of cut flowers. They weren't wrapped in cellophane or thick, decorative paper, as they would have been had they come from a florist, but were tied together by a rough piece of string. They showed no signs of drooping, so they were either freshly picked or had recently been in water.

"These just came," Harvey said. "For Audrey Ashley. I thought you wouldn't mind giving them to her. I have no idea where she is. I would have asked Aaron to deliver them, but he's not answering my texts, and I have no idea where he is, either. I think he's avoiding me."

"No problem," said Charlotte. "I'll see that she gets them." She lifted the bundle of roses up by their stems, ran her hand under them, and then looked around the desk. "Did they come with a card to say who they're from?"

"No. They came just like that."

"Well, did you see anybody drop them off? Do you know who sent them?"

"How should I know?" Harvey said with an impatient shrug. "I just came out here a few minutes ago and there they were, lying on the counter, just as you saw them."

"Well, how do you know they're for Audrey, then?"

Harvey raised his eyebrows. "I just assumed. Who else would be getting flowers? And all the other ones were for her. Why wouldn't these ones be?"

"Wait a minute. When you say, 'all the other ones' and 'they come just like that'—so this isn't the first time?"

"No, there have been several bunches like that, so I just send Aaron down to her bungalow with them."

"It's not a good idea to keep delivering these to Audrey," Charlotte said. "And anyway, they're not addressed to her. Either throw them out or find a vase and put them somewhere here in the lobby."

"I'll take them to Nancy's office. She'll know what to do with them. Maybe she'd like them. They're nice roses."

"Yes, they are nice roses. On second thought, I'll take them. But I won't be giving them to Audrey."

"Why not?"

"Because someone's been sending her flowers anonymously, and there's something a bit creepy about it."

"I thought women liked getting flowers."

"They do. I mean, we do, but only if we know who they're from. Otherwise, it's unsettling, wondering who sent them. There's the person we wish they were from, and then there's the person they're really from. Who usually turns out to be someone you don't want sending you flowers."

"Well, I'll leave it with you to do what you want. You know more about these things than I do." He turned to enter the door behind the reception desk that led to his office, stopped, and turned around again. "I meant to ask you. Did you get all that business sorted out about the director and the play? Nancy wasn't very happy about that. You know how she feels about anything that might reflect badly on the hotel."

"If you're talking about the Civil War version of the play, I think Nancy'll find it does the hotel a world of good in terms of publicity," Charlotte said. "As for the director, yes, it was very unfortunate about the English director, but we've got a replacement in place, a local fellow, and the cast seem to really like him, so everything's fine. In fact, they're rehearsing now, and from what I can see, there's no reason why the play shouldn't open on time. I mean, it has to."

"Well, that's good," said Harvey. "We're booked solid almost all fall. But you'll keep me informed if anything happens, I hope. I hate being the last to know. Nobody ever tells me anything."

Charlotte gathered up the flowers and set off for her office. She filled a vase with water and gave the flowers a drink while she examined them and thought about what to do. They were superior to supermarket flowers and comparable to florist roses. Except if they'd come from a florist, they'd have been wrapped in a more presentable way, and the delivery wouldn't have been secretive. Most likely, they were homegrown, and she had a good idea whose garden they came from.

But first, she wanted to find out how many more bouquets like them Audrey had received. She scooped the flowers out of their vase and wrapped their dripping stems in a plastic bag. After stopping off at her bungalow long enough to get Rupert, the two set off for the star bungalow.

Rupert remained on the path, watching her, while she climbed the stairs and knocked on the door. "Just a minute," called a voice from within. A moment later, Maxine opened the door, met Charlotte's eyes, and lowered her gaze to take in the flowers she was holding. "Oh," she said in a flat tone. "More of those. We're running out of vases."

"May we come in?"

"Of course."

Maxine led the way to the sitting room, where several similar flower arrangements stood on windowsills and tables. Rupert gave a little growl at Maxine and then sat down beside the sofa.

"I was just about to toss that one," Maxine said, reaching for a vase whose flowers sat in pale-green water. The roses' petals, once a dark pink, were beginning to turn brown around the edges and curled in. A few petals had dropped and fallen on the table.

"How often do the flowers arrive?" Charlotte asked.

"Every few days. There are more in Audrey's bedroom."

"Still no idea who's sending them?"

Maxine shook her head. "At first, she thought it might be Edmund, but now, of course, she knows it couldn't have been him because they just keep coming. In fact, I think she even got a bunch the night he died." She hunched up her shoulders in a vague shrug.

"How and when do they arrive?" Charlotte asked.

"It varies. Sometimes that young man you see about the place, Aaron I think he's called, brings them down from the hotel. Sometimes they're on the steps when I leave in the morning."

"When you leave?"

"I take an early morning walk for about an hour. I set off as soon as it's light so I'm back in time to prepare Audrey's breakfast and make sure she's up and has everything she needs for the day."

"I see. And the ones that are left on your door step—I guess they don't come with a card or anything?"

Maxine shook her head. "But you have to understand, this kind of thing is really common for popular actresses. Happens all the time. Goes with the territory."

"I'm well aware of that. And sometimes the actress feels it's really creepy and annoying, and other times she's flattered. When I first talked to Audrey, she didn't seem to mind. I wondered how she's feeling about it now."

"To be honest, she's had enough of it. She wishes whoever's doing this would stop."

"I think that would be a very good idea. Shall I tell you how to make it stop?"

Maxine nodded.

"Get rid of them. All of them."

Maxine tilted her head.

"You can see the flowers in their vases through the window. I've seen them on my dog walks. That sends a message to whoever is sending them that you like them enough to display them. Once he gets the message that you don't like them or want them, he'll stop sending them."

Maxine's mouth twitched to one side while she thought that over. "That makes sense."

"So let's get them all bagged up, and I'll take them away with me." Maxine disappeared into a bedroom and returned with a distinctive dark-green bag from a famous London department store. "Seems such a waste of a good bag," she said as they lifted the flowers from the vases, bent the stems in two, and stuffed them in the bag. "But I suppose it's worth it."

Charlotte and Rupert walked back to her bungalow, where she phoned Paula. "I've got some flowers here," Charlotte said, "and you need to take a look at them. I've got to get back to work now, but is there any chance you can drop in later?"

*

"Yes, they certainly look like they're from my garden," Paula said when Charlotte showed her the flowers that had been left at the hotel's front desk. She reached into the bag and pulled out a cream-colored rose with a pink tint on the edge of its petals. "These grow in the bed beneath the terrace." She sighed. "I can't believe Ned would do such a thing. It seems so out of character. Well, I'll talk to him, and if it was him, now that he knows we're onto him, it'll stop."

She dropped the flower back in the bag and closed it. "What's the news on the Edmund Albright front? Are they any closer to knowing what happened?"

"They think they are," said Charlotte, "but I don't agree with them."

Paula sank into a chair, and Charlotte offered her a glass of sparkling mineral water with ice and a slice of lemon. "Tell me," said Paula as she reached for it.

"The police say it's a 'likely' suicide and don't seem interested in investigating. They seem to rely so much on forensics, but they don't think about the circumstances surrounding it. We know Edmund wasn't in a suicidal frame of mind. And Ray himself said it wasn't an accident, so that can only leave . . ."

"Murder."

Chapter 19

Aaron was bent over the worktable, focused and intent on the documents laid out in front of him, when Charlotte and Rupert arrived the next morning. On days when her handsome corgi asked to go to work with her, she almost always agreed, and she kept a dog basket beside her desk for him.

"Morning."

Aaron looked up from his work. "Oh, hi, Charlotte. I've finished the sketches for Beatrice and Hero. If you want to look them over, and they're okay, we can show them to Wade."

"Just let me get Rupert settled." She unclipped his leash so he could explore the workroom and make sure everything was just as he left it on his last visit. Once reassured that everything was in order, he climbed into his basket, where he could keep a watchful eye on the office comings and goings.

Aaron arranged his sketches. Each featured a few words of explanation—such as *chemise* or *V-shaped bodice* with an arrow pointing to a section of the garment—and had a couple of fabric swatches pinned to them. Charlotte fingered a fabric attached to a Hero sketch. "I don't really like the color. It's too dark and heavy. She's young and innocent, so you want something that will convey that to the audience. And we have to think about the size of the skirts. If they're too full, they're going to need elaborate crinolines or even a hoopskirt to hold them out. And they'll take up too much room onstage and be difficult for the actresses to move in, so you'll need to make some adjustments there. But other than that, they look fine. And when Wade's approved them, you can get to work. In the meantime, I'll get the men in and measure them up so I can order their costumes." She referred to her notes. "One South and half a dozen North."

Aaron shuffled his sketches into order, then walked to his desk and held up the latest issue of *American Theater* magazine. "Remember Simon Dyer?"

"Of course I remember Simon bloody Dyer."

"This came this morning, and you might want to take a look at it."

"Just tell me."

"He's been appointed artistic director at some fancy theater and performing arts center in Colorado."

"It figures."

Neither said anything for a moment, and then Aaron placed the magazine on Charlotte's desk. "I'd better go. Wade wants me at the rehearsal this morning."

"We're going to be desperately busy for the next couple of weeks. Right, on your bike, then."

She puttered around the office, picking up scraps of cloth that had fallen off the worktable and emptying the recycling bin in the tiny kitchen. Her gaze drifted often to the magazine on her desk, and she had just picked it up and started leafing through to the appointments section when the door opened and Mattie slunk in. Charlotte lowered the magazine to her lap and met Mattie's eyes. Normally impish and bright, they were dull and downcast. Her hair, which she often wore scraped back in a neat ponytail, was tied loosely over one shoulder and carelessly braided.

"Hi, Mattie. I can see you're still worried."

"I can't believe how stupid I was. How naïve."

"Do you know for sure yet?" Mattie shook her head in distress. "Want my advice?" Mattie nodded. "Get yourself down to the drugstore, love, get yourself a kit, and find out for sure so you can decide what to do."

They sat in an uneasy silence as faint sounds of actors' voices in rehearsal drifted down the corridor and through the open door. Mattie sighed. "I don't know what I came in here for, really; just needed someone to talk to, I guess." She wrapped the curl on the end of her braid around a finger and twisted it as she glanced at Charlotte through sideways eyes. "I just wondered if there was any news on Edmund. Have the police decided for sure it was suicide?"

"I believe it's the medical examiner's office that makes the final decision on manner of death," said Charlotte, "and it's my understanding that, yes, they will classify it as a suicide."

Charlotte couldn't quite read Mattie's reaction. A faint smile twitched at the corners of her mouth, but disappeared, replaced by a light frown.

"Everybody's been talking about it," Mattie said. "Is it too much to ask that we put that behind us and move on? We don't need the memory of him hovering over us like Banquo's ghost."

"When you were with Edmund, did he give you any indications that he was upset or worried about anything?" Charlotte asked.

Mattie let out a weak little laugh. "No. But what do I know? I really didn't spend that much time with him." She stood up, and as she did, a puzzled look flashed across her face. Her eyes widened as she placed a hand on her abdomen, and without saying anything, she ran out of the room.

A few minutes later, she was back, a huge grin creasing her face. She hugged Charlotte and said, "It's here. Everything's all right now."

"You must be so relieved! I'm so glad. A complication like that on top of everything else is the last thing we need right now."

"Thanks for listening. Talk to you later." Mattie tossed her hair over her shoulder as she skipped from the room.

*

"Mrs. Van Dusen, Ned wants to speak to you." Paula Van Dusen's housekeeper hovered in the doorway of her study. Seated on her butterscotch-colored leather sofa with Coco, her corgi pup, curled up asleep beside her, Paula took off her reading glasses and lowered the theater financial statements she'd been examining.

"I suppose he wants to talk to me outside."

The housekeeper smiled. "Yes, he said if you don't mind, he'll wait for you outside." She gestured at the window that overlooked the driveway. "His boots and clothes are dirty, and he doesn't want to track garden muck all over the carpets. He's at the front door."

Paula rose, placed the documents on her tidy desk, and, accompanied by the housekeeper, walked down the corridor and through the great front hall. "Coco just woke up, so she should go out. Would you tell Barnes I'd like him to walk her in the garden for ten minutes?" she asked as the housekeeper opened the front door and stood to one side. Paula stepped outside to be greeted by Ned, holding his flat cap in both hands, frowning anxiously.

His gray hair curled over his collar, and his chin was covered in stubble that almost matched the coarse hair that sprouted from his large ears. No one had ever seen him dressed in anything other than serviceable denim gardening overalls. In summer, he wore a faded cotton check shirt; in spring and fall, he wore a flannel check shirt under a dark-green sleeveless down vest that his late wife had bought him decades ago.

"Good morning, Ned," said Paula. "Got your vest on, I see."

"Morning, Mrs. Van Dusen. Yes, the weather's starting to turn."

"You wanted to talk to me, I believe."

Ned took a step closer and looked around before speaking. "I wanted to talk to you about the flowers."

"Yes, and I wanted to talk to you too about the flowers. I'm very interested to hear what you've got to say. It's about the roses, isn't it?"

"Well, the roses, and there's other flowers too."

"Yes, so I gathered. What about them, Ned? What would you like to tell me?"

He shifted his weight from one foot to the other, took a deep, dreary sigh, and fixed his gaze somewhere on the horizon.

"The fall fair's coming up in a few weeks."

"Yes, I'm aware of that, Ned." She crossed her arms and waited for his eyes to drift back to her. When they didn't, she spoke. "Look, Ned, let's stop beating about the bush and get to the point, shall we? You want to tell me something about the roses. Now why don't you just come out with it. And look at me, please, when you're speaking to me."

"I thought you should know. Someone's been stealing our flowers, including the buds that would have matured just in time for the flower show. So I don't know what I'm going to do about this year's entries for the fair."

Paula's eyes widened as she let out a little gasp and touched her lips with her fingertips. "Did you just say someone's been stealing our roses? Do you mean it wasn't you who took them?"

Now it was Ned's turn to look surprised. "Me? Steal my own flowers?" He shook his head mournfully. "Not me. I started noticing flowers going missing a month or so back.

At first I thought someone was cutting them for the house, although they shouldn't be, so I went 'round to the kitchen door and spoke to the housekeeper. She asked everybody, and nobody from inside the house has been cutting them. At least nobody's owning up to it."

"But the house is gated, so someone can't be sneaking into the garden and helping themselves. It must be an inside job, Ned."

"That's what I thought."

"I'm sure you've been thinking about this. Do you have any idea who it could be?"

"Well, I don't want to speak out of turn or get anybody in trouble, you know, but there is someone it could be."

As he spoke, Barnes came around the corner of the building with Coco dancing at his heels. Ned's blue eyes followed Barnes's progress and then returned to meet Paula's, with the slightest tip of his head.

"Thank you, Ned. I'm glad we had this little chat. That'll be all for now."

"Very good, Mrs. Van Dusen." Ned walked away with his back slightly bowed even though he wasn't bent over his wheelbarrow. He passed Barnes going in the opposite direction, but neither man spoke.

Seeing Paula, Coco ran toward her. Paula leaned over, patted her, and waited for Barnes to catch up with her. "Barnes, I would like to see you in my study in ten minutes, please." She opened the door and Coco scampered inside, with Paula close behind.

*

"Barnes?" Charlotte's eyes widened. "It was Barnes?"

"Yes, I'm afraid poor old Barnes has been sending the flowers to Audrey," said Paula. "He only meant to send her the one bouquet when she first arrived, but then he got carried away, and to keep the costs down, he started helping himself to the flowers from the Oakland gardens. He didn't think they'd be missed."

Paula let out a little exclamation of dismay. "Oh, poor Barnes. He's a bit old to be mooning around like some lovesick creature. Imagine him out in the garden, picking flowers in the dead of night, and dropping them off here. For all I know, he's been hanging around here, hoping to catch a glimpse of her."

"If it weren't so awful, it would be quite sad, really."

"Yes. He was terribly embarrassed during out little chat. Said he didn't know what had come over him. That he'd been a big fan of hers for years and just felt drawn to her in this way." Paula squeezed lime juice into her glass and dropped the crushed wedge into her drink. "I told him that since Audrey hadn't lodged a formal complaint that the matter would go no further but that it must stop." Charlotte nodded her agreement. "I also told him that he must apologize to Ned. He's picked all Ned's best blooms for the flower show, and Ned's devastated.

"He knows every bloom and every leaf in that garden—especially this time of year, when he's keeping a close eye on what he's going to enter at the fair."

Charlotte straightened in her chair. "Is this the first time Barnes has done something like this? I mean, let's be honest and call it what it was. He was stalking her, and that's a serious offense. I don't think men realize how unsettling that is for a woman. And it isn't just the flowers. Audrey said she thought someone was lurking outside her home, and Ray got called out twice, I think it was, in the middle of the night to check it out and reassure her. At the time, he and I kind of laughed it off, thinking she was making it up as an excuse to lure him over to her bungalow, but now I wonder. If Barnes was spying on her, peering in her windows, let's say, that's serious compared to just sending her flowers. I didn't mention the flowers to Ray. But I wonder now if I should have. Barnes is actually really lucky that I didn't tell him."

"Yes, he is," Paula agreed. "And I told him so. As far as I know, he's never done anything like this before. I believed him when he said he simply got carried away."

"You're sure he understands that what he did was wrong? That he really gets it?"

"I'm sure he does, and I'm confident it won't happen again."

"Let's hope not. Because if he does it again, we will have no choice but to report it. And we might end up in trouble because we didn't report it this time."

Chapter 20

The play began to take shape as actors and the director explored the words, discovering hidden depths of meaning, and related their insights to the time period during which they were setting the play. As the most populous state in the North, New York sent more officers, men, and supplies to the Union army than any other state. Director Wade Radcliffe, who now saw the concept as a rich vein to be mined, and the designers adapted a couple of sets to depict a chapel and an upstate home befitting the character of a prosperous Leonato. Wade, Charlotte, and Aaron finalized costuming and, tasked with creating the women's costumes, Aaron was busier than he'd ever been. His sewing machine had been humming for days as he stitched skirts, tops, and dresses. The uniforms for the male actors had arrived, and costume fittings were about to begin, with the start of dress rehearsals just a few days away.

"Audrey will be here for her first costume fitting soon," Charlotte reminded Aaron first thing on an early autumn morning. "I'm just going to take a final look at her dress." Aaron did not look up from his sewing but kept his eyes on the fabric as he guided it through the machine. Finally, when he approached the end of the seam, he gently raised his foot from the pedal to slow the needle and then stopped. He lifted the presser foot, turned the fabric, and lowered it before turning to speak to Charlotte.

"Sorry. Just wanted to finish that. Yes, her costume is ready for the first fitting. I finished the detailing last night. Will she be hard to please, do you think?"

"I'm not sure, to be honest. The one who could be hard to please is Maxine. She keeps a close eye on everything to do with Audrey's professional life and, as you may have noticed, is very protective of her. She's worried that the dress won't be flattering. You've had a real challenge to come up with something period appropriate and age appropriate without being matronly. I can't wait to hear how you did that. Let's go over it together, and you can talk me through it in case we have to explain it to Audrey."

The dress, which was actually a skirt and matching bodice, was fitted on a mannequin, covered in a dust sheet. Aaron gently lifted the protective covering off the garment, and the two stood back and surveyed it. It was made of a sturdy cotton in a dark-green pattern of checks with a plain collar. The lined bodice included a row of tiny buttons down the front. The full skirt, which had not yet been hemmed, featured squares of a larger plaid, which had been appliquéd to form a diamond pattern, about eighteen inches from the floor. "That worked out well," said Charlotte, pointing at it. "Now what are we going to do about crinolines? How big will the skirt be?" she made a circular, puffy motion by swinging her hands around her hips.

"I'll talk to Audrey and see how big she wants it. My suggestion will be big enough to add a bit of volume, but not so big as to restrict movement."

"That's right. We're not doing *The King and I*." Charlotte checked her watch. "They're due in a few minutes."

"I learned a lot, actually, by sitting in on rehearsals and listening to what the actors had to say about their characters," said Aaron. "I didn't realize that actors focus on what their character is doing in the moment, while the director worries about the big picture. I hadn't thought of a play in that light before. And what I picked up from watching Audrey in rehearsal is how sharp her Beatrice character is. Definitely ahead of her time but still mindful of her position in Leonato's household. So I thought about what kind of clothes she would wear. She would wear something traditional, but maybe just a little edgy, so I tried to design a dress that should move well with her. That's the most important part, besides the silhouette, of course."

As he finished speaking, a flurry of activity at the door announced the arrival of Audrey and her sister.

"Only us!" Maxine called out.

"Come in," said Charlotte. "Aaron's finished your main costume, Audrey. We'll dress it up with a shawl and bonnet for the outdoor scenes, and once we see how it fits, we'll whip up a fairly similar one for the wedding scene. If you'd like to go 'round behind the screen and try it on, we'll get started. You'll find a petticoat there for you."

Aaron removed the skirt and bodice from the mannequin and placed them gently in Maxine's outstretched arms. She and Audrey disappeared behind the screen. Aaron crossed his arms, glanced at Charlotte, and walked slowly back and forth until Audrey emerged from behind the screen, followed by a scowling Maxine. Audrey walked to the full-length mirror and, turning this way and that as she plumped up the skirt and tugged at the bodice, examined her image.

Charlotte retreated to her office chair as Aaron stepped forward to lead the costume fitting. "Well, what do you think?" he asked.

"It needs more fullness," said Maxine, fussing around Audrey. "More poofiness."

"It's a period day dress, remember, not a ball gown," said Charlotte. "We can add some volume, but not too much."

"She has to move quickly around the other characters," Aaron added. "Audrey, walk around for a bit and get the feel of it. And then we can talk about shoes."

Audrey walked up and down, practiced a few turns, experimented with a few sweeping hand gestures to test how the dress felt along the back and shoulders, and returned to Aaron. "It feels fine," she said.

"And what about the color?" asked Maxine. "She'll look very dull and drab. This looks like something a governess would wear. It would be fine if she was playing Jane Eyre, but she's playing bright, lively Beatrice. What's that girl playing Hero wearing? Something youthful and pretty, I'll bet. We want all eyes on Audrey, and they won't be in that frumpy dress." She folded her arms and glared at Charlotte. "And that row of buttons down the front! It looks ridiculous!"

"If you're as unhappy with the costume as you seem to be, Maxine, we'll need to discuss this with the director. We made this costume with his approval. This is how he envisions Beatrice," Charlotte said, "and presumably, we received our direction after he and Audrey had fully explored the character."

A pink line began to form on Maxine's neck and gradually flushed upward until her face was glowing.

"And about the director," Maxine said, "and this absurd Civil War thing. I thought after Edmund killed himself that that idea would be dropped. It's preposterous that anyone would think of doing such a daft thing."

Audrey shot her a look Charlotte couldn't quite read. "Maxine," Charlotte said in a calm, soothing voice, "the Civil War train has left the station. The costume looks fine, but if you like, we can add a bit of lace on the collar to dress it up. When Aaron's finished with the detailing, it will work very well."

"Well, I'm not so sure," said Maxine, raising her voice. She turned to Audrey. "It doesn't suit you, and I don't think it does you justice."

"I really don't care what you think," Audrey muttered.

"Well, you bloody well should!" Maxine exploded. "You should care very much what I think!"

Chapter 21

"Wow," said Aaron when the sisters had departed. "What do we do now?" He removed his tape measure from around his neck and rolled it up.

"We keep calm and carry on," Charlotte replied. "We've got more fittings coming up and we're going to get on with them. And by the way, you did a terrific job on that costume, so don't take what Maxine said personally. You did exactly what you were asked to do, and you did it professionally and skillfully." She frowned. "I must say, Maxine was really wound up, wasn't she? I wonder what that was really about."

"She thought the dress didn't suit her sister?"

"I got the feeling there was more to it. There's a tension there."

Aaron carried the disputed garment back to its mannequin and arranged it carefully, brushing his hand down the row of navy-blue buttons down the front. "I was a bit hurt she didn't like the buttons," he said. "I thought they were a nice decorative detail. I put a lot of thought into them." The buttons were not used to actually open and close the garment; strips of Velcro sewn on a band behind them allowed for easy opening of the bodice to facilitate a quick costume change, and having the fastening at the front rather than the back meant the actress could handle costume changes herself rather than having to rely on a dresser. "Audrey left before I could measure the hem length. She'll have to come back for a second fitting."

"Hopefully she can leave Maxine at home next time. We don't need her negativity." Charlotte checked her workbook for the list of fittings scheduled for the day. "The rest of the morning is free and then lots of fittings this afternoon, including Mattie."

Aaron wheeled the mannequin out of the way, positioned it against the wall, and draped the sheet over it. "That's because they're all at rehearsal this morning. It's the wedding scene. Mattie's wedding dress is almost finished, and I've got time to work on it now so it's ready for her fitting this afternoon."

"Okay, you do that. I'm going to sit in on the rehearsal."

Theater rehearsal rooms are almost always closed to outsiders. They're meant to be safe places where actors can try on a role and wear it for an hour or a day, experiment, do anything and everything to find the heart and voice of a role, make mistakes, and indulge in whimsy and nonsense until they understand where their character has come from and what he seeks and why he wants it. They do this by playing off other actors, and gradually, as they work out the mechanics of the play and the technical aspects, it comes together as the words are lifted off their pages and take on a life of their own.

Charlotte paused outside the rehearsal room and cracked open the door an inch or two. Hearing Wade speaking to the cast, she slipped into the room, closing the door quietly behind her. She moved along the wall, maneuvered her way around a bicycle, and stood between it and the piano, listening.

"As we've discussed before, gender politics is central to this play," said Wade, "and in no place is that more evident than in the aborted wedding scene. When Claudio thinks Hero has been unfaithful to him, he humiliates and rejects her and then refuses to marry her. And as if that weren't bad enough for Hero, her own father, Leonato, sides with Claudio and wishes his daughter dead for the shame she has brought to the house."

While he paused to let the effect of his words sink in, Charlotte looked at Mattie, who was playing Hero. Her eyes were shining, and she was hanging on Wade's every word. Charlotte could almost see the wheels spinning as Mattie processed what this could mean to the way she played this scene. Charlotte's attention moved on to Audrey, who was studying her fingernails. After losing interest in them, she gazed at the clock above the door, and when her eyes met Charlotte's, she gave her an ingratiating smile. Charlotte realized that she wasn't paying attention because Wade wasn't talking about her.

"And how this wedding scene is played will affect how the audience will view the ending of the play, when, her innocence having been proved, Hero agrees to marry Claudio, despite his earlier treatment of her. What does this mean? Does the audience think the couple will live happily ever after? Will a modern audience, and modern women particularly, accept the marriage? Or will they think she should reject him?"

He looked around the cast. "Well, let's play it out, shall we, and see what happens. Let's have Hero and Claudio, here"—he motioned to the two actors—"and Leonato and the friar over here, and the rest of you bring chairs behind them as if you were in the chapel." He leaned over and exchanged a few words with the actor playing Claudio. "Right. Places, everyone. Now remember, Claudio has been tricked into thinking he saw Hero being unfaithful to him, and everybody has gathered in the church for the ceremony where he and Hero are expected to marry. And let's begin."

The scene begins with a light exchange and continues as Claudio interrupts the friar, who is conducting the service, to ask Hero's father if he gives his daughter freely in marriage. When Leonato replies he does, Claudio responds, "There, Leonato, take her back again."

And with that, the actor playing Claudio grabbed Mattie by her upper arm and flung her away from him. Mattie, not expecting to be thrown so roughly, cried out as the actor playing Leonato reached out for her.

"Keep going!" shouted Wade. The emotion intensified, and Mattie, caught up in the moment, gave a chilling performance, filled with fear and confusion, punctuated by real tears. When it was over, the cast stood up and applauded. Audrey, Charlotte noticed, was just that little bit slower to rise, her smile seemed forced and insincere for all her acting skills, and her applause seemed halfhearted, as if she were performing an unpleasant task that was expected of her.

"Well done," said Wade. "I think we're ready to move out of this cloistered rehearsal room and onto the stage. What do you think? Are you up for it?"

Cast members nodded eagerly in agreement. "Good for you," Wade said. "Normally we'd spend at least four weeks in a rehearsal room, and we haven't had anything like that, so to move this quickly is exceptional. You've all done a wonderful job. Let's leave it there for this morning. Some of you have your first costume fittings this afternoon, and I know you'll enjoy that. Let's go for lunch and we can talk there. I don't know about you, but I'm starved."

The cast filed out and Charlotte stayed behind to pick up the water bottles they'd left behind. She found a copy of the script and a red sweater draped on a chair, but she left them where they were, assuming that sooner or later they'd be missed and their owners would return looking for them.

She sat in one of the plastic chairs and thought about the scene she'd just watched. Mattie had given an astonishing performance and had really seemed to lose herself in this character. Charlotte wondered if Wade had been coaching her. Would Mattie have been able to achieve something like that under Edmund's direction?

And the way the cast was responding to Wade, it was as if Edmund's short time here had never happened. From a crushing disappointment at not getting the appointment that had originally gone to Edmund, to now be leading the cast into what could very well turn into a hit, Wade had certainly made his mark.

Charlotte stood up and, after taking one last look around the room, closed the door behind her, dropped the water bottles into a recycling bin, and left the hotel by the back door. On the short walk to her bungalow, her thoughts returned to Mattie and Wade. Both had benefitted from Edmund's death. Wade had got the directing job he wanted, and Mattie had found herself rid of a man in the position to cause her embarrassment now and possibly scandal later in her career. But had either benefitted enough to want him dead?

And what about Barnes, who adored Audrey? Had he seen or heard Edmund mistreating Audrey in some way that had prompted him to lash out at Edmund? Had he gone to see him, argued with him, somehow got hold of the gun, and used it to kill Edmund?

And then there was Nancy, who feared a Civil War–themed production could hurt the hotel's reputation and, if bookings dropped, could even mean she was laid off again.

Who had the most to lose? Charlotte thought. Or, to put it another way, who had the most to gain from Edmund's death?

Chapter 22

After walking Rupert and eating a quick bowl of soup, Charlotte returned to her workroom, where Aaron was setting up for the afternoon fittings. Without any coaching from Charlotte, he'd come up with the idea of creating a mourning dress for Hero's waiting-gentlewoman, explaining to Charlotte that since the play was set after a war, there would have been casualties, and having a minor character dressed in black would reinforce that message. Charlotte had been impressed that he'd thought of that.

So when she opened the workroom door, two dresses in stark contrast awaited her. One black, one white. She examined them. The black one was made of a dull cotton, had no trim, and was plain and functional. The white garment, however—Hero's wedding dress—was a frothy feast for the eyes. The bodice ended in a tightly fitted waist, and the bell-shaped skirt flared into several rows of organza flounces. Underneath was a stiff petticoat.

"This costume might have to accommodate some rough stage action," Charlotte said when Aaron showed it to her. "Claudio got a bit physical with Hero in the rehearsal today, so you have to make sure it's not too tight, especially across the back. It would be awful if it tore." Aaron winced. "It would be difficult to repair in a hurry. If we had more time, and in a perfect world, we'd have a backup."

One by one, the cast members filed in for their fittings. Some took longer than others, as Aaron and Charlotte discussed the garments with each actor. Charlotte was amused that Aaron had adopted a contemplative stance from the cohost of a popular clothing-design reality show, standing with his left hand clasping his right elbow and resting his chin on his right fist while he frowned and pondered the actor in front of him. Notes were made and pinned to each costume indicating the necessary adjustments, and the garments were hung on a separate rack ready for Aaron's attention in the morning.

At 4:00 PM, on time and accompanied by Wade Radcliffe, Mattie entered the costume department. "I just want to make sure the dress will hold up in the scene," Wade said. "As you saw, we're going to play it with robustness."

"It was impressive. I explained the situation to Aaron." She pulled out a chair, gestured to Wade to sit, and the fitting was under way. Twenty minutes later, the dress was declared a success, Wade left, and Mattie, once more wearing street clothes, was ready to leave. Charlotte glanced at Aaron, who was fussing over the dress.

"All finished for the day, are you, Mattie?" Charlotte asked.

"Yes, I am. You?"

"Oh, I think I could be, if it's okay with Aaron." Aaron nodded his approval and went back to his dress. "Right, then, see you in the morning."

Charlotte and Mattie walked down the hall toward the cafeteria.

"It's a beautiful day," said Mattie. "Would you like to go for a walk?"

"I like walking," said Charlotte, "but I don't see any point to it unless I've got Rupert. We'll stop off and collect him, if that's all right with you." A few minutes later, with Rupert scurrying ahead of them, they entered the acre or so of parkland that bordered the hotel. It was familiar to Rupert, and he ran ahead to check out favorite smells.

"I wanted to ask you something," Charlotte said as they watched the puffy fur on his back legs, "about Edmund." Mattie let out a little groan. "When you and he . . . well, did you get the feeling that he was practiced at that sort of thing . . . that you weren't the first?"

"Seducing a young actress, you mean?"

"That's exactly what I mean."

"Yes, I did."

"And afterward, how did he leave it? Did he ask you not to tell anyone?"

Mattie thought for a moment. "No, I don't think he did. I think he knew that I wouldn't dream of telling anyone, because it would make me look as stupid as I felt." After a moment, she added, "I hadn't thought about that before, but now that you mention it, it was the other way 'round. It was more like I was afraid *he* would tell someone. And he sensed that was how I felt. I can't remember his exact words, but he said something to let me know he had something he could hold over me."

"And how did that make you feel?"

"Well, as you can imagine, I felt threatened. It was really unpleasant. I felt dirty—violated even, to be honest." Mattie shuddered. "Now can we please talk about something else? What did you think of the wedding scene rehearsal?"

"It was wonderful. You really infused it with a lot of emotion. I got the sense that you've been discussing your part with Wade."

"It was you, really, who showed me what the part could be, and then I talked to him. I've learned so much from him. Much more than I ever would have learned from Edmund. All he cared about was himself and what this play could mean for his career."

They had passed the director's empty bungalow, with its dark, lifeless windows. Mattie stopped and gazed back at it. "Strange to think he died in there," she said, then faced forward and continued walking. "Do you think his body's been shipped home yet or whatever they do with it?"

"I don't know, to be honest," said Charlotte. "He could have been cremated, I suppose, and his ashes returned to his family. Maybe there'll be a service for him in Stratford." They were now approaching the star bungalow. A slight swinging motion at the edge of the curtain indicated that someone had been looking out the window and then dropped the curtain as Charlotte and Mattie approached. "And how are you getting on with Audrey?" Charlotte asked. "Everything all right there?"

"I'm not sure," said Mattie. "At first she seemed as if she wanted to help me, but when she says her lines with me, they're mechanical and don't really give me much to work off. And yet when she's acting with the actor playing Benedick, there's the liveliness you expect. Of course it's just rehearsal, so she may be holding back, but Wade has asked everyone to put it all out there. There's something about her that just seems fake. Even when she's not acting, she's acting, if you know what I mean."

"Interesting," commented Charlotte. They had reached the end of the path, and Charlotte called Rupert to her to turn around for the walk home. They walked along in silence, Rupert leading the way. As they reached the star bungalow, Maxine hurried toward them.

"Charlotte," she said, "I wondered if I might have a word."

"Of course," Charlotte smiled at her. Maxine folded her arms and found something of interest at her feet. When she said nothing more, Mattie got the message.

"Right," she said. "Thanks for the walk, Charlotte." She gave Rupert a friendly pat around the ears, then remarked casually to both women, "See you around."

Maxine watched Mattie's retreating back, and when she judged the young woman to be far enough away, she spoke. "We've had some good news. Exciting news, actually. The *New York Times* wants to do a piece on Audrey. Well, at least that man, what's his name, the local reporter . . ."

"Fletcher Macmillan?"

"Yes, that's the one. Apparently he writes occasional articles for the *New York Times*, and he's going to do a story on Audrey. So the thing is, they're sending a photographer tomorrow, and they want some shots of her in costume. Will her dresses be ready?" It wasn't really a question; it was an order.

"Yes, of course. Where is the shoot taking place? Will you pick up the costumes in my department, or do you want Aaron to deliver them somewhere?"

"If he could just have them in Audrey's dressing room by nine o'clock, we'll take it from there. The final details haven't exactly been arranged. I don't know if they'll want a theater-type setting or . . ." She gestured toward the woods. "They might want something out here. Bucolic. Pastoral. Something along those lines."

Tree hugging. Something along those lines, Charlotte thought. *It's been done before, I believe.*

"That's fine," she said with what she hoped passed for a sincere smile. "You can let me know tomorrow if you need my help with anything."

"Oh, that's very kind of you to offer, but we'll manage. I've been looking after Audrey for a long time. I know how she likes things done, and I take care of her hair and makeup."

She looked at Rupert, who had been sitting quietly a little way off, waiting and watching. He strolled closer to Charlotte and stood beside her, his dark, furry body leaning protectively against her leg.

*

The next morning, Aaron unlocked the door to the star dressing room. Located to give easy access to the backstage area, the dressing room had benefitted from a modest makeover. At Maxine's request, it had been painted a soft cream; the lighting surrounding the makeup mirror had been updated; the portable costume rack had been replaced with a smaller, newer one; and every effort had been made to ensure the room was clean and comfortable. The window opened to let in fresh air, a feature many dressing rooms—often located in the bowels of a theater—did not have.

Theater dressing rooms are as individual as the actors who occupy them. Some are messy and lived-in, others are neat, clean, and tidy. Audrey's was pristine. Without turning on the overhead lights, Aaron hung Audrey's costumes on the rack. He'd been up late the night before, finishing them with hand stitching and careful pressing. As he smoothed the skirts and then stepped back to examine them, he was pleased with the result. After sliding one costume just a little farther down the rail so it couldn't touch the skirt of the one beside it, he entered the bathroom to change Audrey's towels. She had asked for new white ones when she arrived, and it was one of his jobs to make sure a plentiful supply was always on hand. He scooped the used ones off the rail, replaced them with fresh ones, and after cleaning the sink, was about to leave when he heard voices approaching from the hall.

"Stop going on about it," said an irritated female voice that Aaron recognized as Maxine's. "It's over and done with. How many times?" The approaching footsteps stopped. "Oh, that's not good. The door's open. I know I locked it last night. I always check to make sure it's locked. If the cleaners left it open, that was very careless of them, and I intend to complain."

"It's all right," said Aaron, emerging from the bathroom. "I unlocked it. I'm just dropping off Audrey's dresses." At the severe frown from Maxine, he corrected himself. "Sorry. Miss Ashley's dresses." Maxine flipped on the light switch, flooding the room with a white fluorescent light as Audrey entered. She placed a cup of tea on the dressing table and turned her back to Maxine, who helped her off with a light-beige Burberry raincoat.

"Miss Ashley's got to get ready for a photo shoot, so you'll have to excuse us," Maxine said to Aaron. "The photographer is due in an hour." Audrey sat at the dressing table and switched on the three rows of bright lights that surrounded the makeup mirror as Aaron edged toward the door. A moment later, Maxine closed the door quietly but firmly behind him.

Chapter 23

With its heightened sense of excitement and expectation, the second-most intense performance of a play, after opening night, is the first dress rehearsal. The company sees for the first time how well blocking and rehearsal, costume design and fittings, and set and lighting design come together, as well as how all the backstage work—artistic and technical—showcase the play and allow the actors to shine in their center stage roles as the face of the drama.

As the play's director, Wade Radcliffe had a busy afternoon ahead of him. The time for discussion and experimentation was over, and it was now time to lock in the production, so any changes would have to be small ones. Aaron would oversee the matinee dress rehearsal production backstage while Charlotte and Wade watched from the aisle seats where the exit sign overhead provided just enough light for them to make notes. Also in the audience would be local high school students and senior citizens, happy to snap up tickets at discount prices and fill seats.

As curtain time approached, the actors assembled backstage. A few went through the comforting little rituals they performed before they took the stage; others stood off by themselves, clearing their minds of everything but the performance ahead of them.

And then, Aaron made the announcement asking the audience to take their seats because the performance was about to begin. He stood beside the curtain, watching the countdown light turn from red to green, and when it did, he pressed the button to open the curtain. He then scurried to his seat at the prompt desk, and the drama began.

Although the play was running smoothly, Charlotte could sense Wade concentrating intently on the stage business, leaning forward at moments that concerned him, and scratching notes on the yellow legal pad on his lap.

As act three, scene one ended, Mattie, playing Hero, exchanged a few lines with the actress playing Ursula, and then, with Mattie leading the way, the two women exited the stage. A moment later, the sound of a heavy thud filled the theater, followed by a sharp cry of pain and then a low, unearthly moan. Wade jumped to his feet, tossed his yellow pad on his seat, and raced up the stairs at the side of the stage to the backstage area.

The audience, unsure what was happening, sat in stunned silence. Charlotte had seen actors injured, and too often, for reasons she could never understand, the audience laughed, thinking it was part of the show. She hurried after Wade to find out what had happened and to offer what help she could.

Mattie was propped up in an awkward, half-sitting position, her weight resting on her right hand and her other hand stretched out to her left ankle. The floor-length skirt of her costume billowed around her calves, revealing her left foot caught in a coil of cabling. As Charlotte arrived, Wade knelt beside Mattie, and a black wing curtain was pushed back, revealing a slightly out-of-breath Aaron.

"What happened?" Aaron asked and then, taking in the scene in front of him, added, "Is Mattie all right?"

No one answered him.

"Aaron should make an announcement and close the curtains," Charlotte said to Wade. He glanced up at her and nodded.

"What do you want me to say?" Aaron asked.

"Tell them there's been an incident backstage and there will be a ten-minute intermission," Charlotte said. "Oh, and apologize, of course."

"And have them bring up the house lights," added Wade.

Mattie reached for Charlotte's hand. "It's my ankle. I must have twisted it. It hurts like hell."

"Do you think you can stand?" Charlotte asked. Having made his announcement, Aaron reappeared with a chair.

"I'll try." Charlotte and Wade lifted her to her feet, and because she could not bear weight on her injured ankle, she hopped the few steps to the chair and sank gratefully onto it. The actress playing Ursula, who had followed Mattie offstage, hovered helplessly nearby.

"What happened?" Wade demanded of her.

"We had just left the stage, and Mattie suddenly took a tumble right in front of me. I grabbed the curtain just in time, or I would have tripped, too, and landed right on top of her."

Mattie pointed to the place where she had fallen. "I tripped on some rope or whatever it is. It shouldn't have been there."

An angry red flush crept up Wade's neck. He walked the few paces to the spot where Mattie had fallen and picked up a coiled length of electrician's cable.

"Aaron," he said in an icy tone, "when the performance is over, I want you to assemble the cast and every member of the crew." He glanced at his watch. "But right now, we've got about five minutes to figure out if the performance can continue or if we should cancel it."

"I don't have that much more stage time," said Mattie. "I'd like to try to finish."

"I wonder if there's a doctor in the house," said Charlotte. "Before Mattie decides if she should continue, we should get a medical opinion. She could make her injured ankle even worse by putting weight on it."

"No," Mattie protested. "Really, I'll be fine. If I can hold onto the actor beside me, I can get through this."

Aaron broke in. "Here's a suggestion. Mattie takes a couple of pain killers now, and for the rest of the play, we find her a chair, and she can sit."

Wade, Charlotte, and Mattie exchanged looks of agreement, and Mattie nodded. "That'll work," she said. "Let's at least give it a try, and I can see a doctor when the play's over."

"I'm sure the audience will understand," agreed Wade. "If no one has a better suggestion, let's do it."

"I'll get some fabric and we can drape a chair to make it look better," said Charlotte. "Good thinking, Aaron. Well done, you!"

*

The performance limped to its conclusion, and for the curtain call, Mattie's chair was arranged in the lineup several actors away from Audrey, who was positioned in the center. Normally, Audrey would have had her moment alone in the warmth of the spotlight, to be swept away on a tidal wave of enthusiastic applause just for her, but because of the logistics of Mattie's injury, the cast acknowledged the audience's accolades as a group one time, the curtain was closed, and the actors prepared to leave the stage.

Mattie remained seated as cast members paused to tell her they hoped she'd be back on her feet in no time, made a couple of 'break a leg' jokes, and dispersed to the dressing rooms to take off their makeup and change into street clothes.

As they disappeared into the wings, Paula Van Dusen climbed the stairs to the stage and took charge of Mattie. "Barnes will drive us to the hospital," she told her, "and I'll stay with you and bring you back. Barnes has gone to get the hotel wheelchair for you, and then we'll be on our way."

When the last audience member had shuffled out of the auditorium, the cast and crew members returned. Following Aaron's instructions, they filled the front rows and sat next to one another; Wade had instructed there were to be no empty seats between them. Flanked by Aaron and Audrey, Charlotte and the rest of the company waited in silence for Wade.

He emerged onstage, hands behind his back, and allowed his eyes to wander over the assembly.

"We had a serious incident during the performance," he began. "Somehow, a length of electrical cable was left on the floor of the wings." He paused for effect and then brought his hands out from behind his back. His right hand held up the cable. "This cable. Does anyone know how it got there?" A murmur rippled through the company. "Somebody's carelessness—if indeed it was a simple act of carelessness—led to Mattie Lane being injured. We were fortunate she wasn't more seriously injured and was able to finish the performance. It could have been much worse. So for all our safety, I ask that you be more aware in the future. And I'm determined to get to the bottom of this and find out who left that cable there. So if you left it there, or you know who did, please let me know."

The hot red flush had crept up his neck again, but his words dripped with a cold suppressed fury that was almost frightening in its intensity. Audrey shifted uncomfortably in her chair, sighed, and glanced at her watch.

"Honestly, what is the point of this?" she whispered to Charlotte. "It's got nothing to do with me. What a waste of time." Charlotte did not reply.

Wade moved on to discussing the performance and praised the company for adapting to the sudden change in staging that Mattie's injury had made necessary. Audrey made a dismissive tsking noise, folded her arms, rolled her eyes, and leaned back in her seat.

A few minutes later, Wade wrapped up and the meeting was over.

"Finally!" exclaimed Audrey, getting to her feet. "Maxine and I are going into town today to order extra copies of this Saturday's *New York Times.* They're running the article about me this weekend." And with that, and without speaking to anyone else, she charged up the aisle and opened the door, passing Paula Van Dusen, who was entering. She glanced back at Audrey, then made her way down the aisle and joined Charlotte.

"Audrey looked like she was in a hurry."

"She didn't like the meeting. Thought it a waste of time. How did you get on with Mattie?" She glanced in the direction of the stage where Wade, having spotted Paula, was hurrying down the stairs. "Never mind. Here comes Wade. You might as well wait until he gets here and then you only have to tell us once."

Still carrying the length of cable, Wade joined them. "Well? How is she? Is anything broken?"

Paula shook her head. "She's got a bad sprain, and they suggested she keep off it for a week or so. They loaned her some crutches. She's gone up to her room to lie down. I'd have her supper sent up on a tray, if I were you."

"Good idea," said Wade. "I'll take it up myself. I want to talk to her about how we're going to get her through the next performances until she's back on her feet. We're going to have to rethink her scenes, especially how she enters and exits."

Charlotte and Paula exchanged a concerned glance, and Paula said, "It would be better if Charlotte took her tray up to her." Wade frowned, so she added, "Perception, Wade. It might look a bit, well . . ."

"Oh, for God's sake," Wade spluttered. "I only offered to take up her meal, but if you want Charlotte to do it, fine."

"It's completely understandable that you need to discuss staging matter with her," said Charlotte. "But surely that can wait until tomorrow. Let her rest."

Wade nodded.

"It would be a good idea if we sent up a tray now," said Paula. "I wonder if she'd like tea or coffee. Plus something sweet." She turned to Charlotte. "What do you think? Cake?"

Before Charlotte could reply, Wade responded with, "She likes tea, with a bit of milk and sugar."

Chapter 24

"I'll walk back to your bungalow with you," said Paula Van Dusen after they had taken Mattie her tea tray. "If that's where you're going now, that is."

"It is. Let's get Rupert and walk."

"I'd like you to tell me what happened when Wade addressed the company. I was sorry I had to miss that."

They walked in silence to Charlotte's bungalow, and then, with Rupert running ahead, Charlotte said, "He showed a side I hadn't seen before. Angry. Seething really, but under control. I think everyone felt a bit unnerved by it. It was unsettling." She turned to Paula. "How well do you know him?"

"Only professionally."

"Have you worked with him before?"

"He did a couple of seasons here a few years back. Well, quite a few years back, I guess. Before your time. And then he moved on."

"He seemed really keen to get this job. When we interviewed him, I was really struck by his intensity and how much this work seemed to mean to him."

"It's very sad for people who work in theater and in films when they reach that point in their careers when the offers dry up and the phone doesn't ring anymore," Paula Van Dusen replied. "So much of their identity is tied up in what they do, it can be hard for many of them to retire. They have egos that need stroking, and it helps them to know that they're still wanted and haven't been forgotten."

"The worst thing, though," said Charlotte, "is when someone younger, and better looking, is getting all the attention that used to be yours."

"Exactly."

"But his contract is just until the end of this run, isn't it?" Charlotte asked.

"Yes. Why?" She gave Charlotte a sharp look.

"I saw something in him today that made me wonder. I asked myself how badly he wanted this job."

"What are you trying to say?"

Charlotte sighed and let out a long, slow breath. "Okay, I'll just come right out and say it. I wonder if he wanted that job bad enough to kill Edmund to get it."

Paula Van Dusen stopped walking and turned to Charlotte. "But he couldn't possibly have known that if Edmund were out of the way, we would offer the job to him. For all he knew, we could have had someone else in mind."

"I don't think so," said Charlotte. "I think he left the interview with us confident he was going to be offered that job, and then Edmund entered the picture and the opportunity Wade wanted so badly was snatched away from him and handed to Edmund. He had to have been bitterly disappointed. But he knew we were short on time, so he might have thought that if somehow, Edmund was no longer in the picture, he'd be in with a chance and we'd offer the director's position to him after all."

"Which is exactly what we did," said Paula. "He knew how desperate we were."

"What he couldn't have known, though, is that the board would want the Civil War version to go ahead. He wasn't happy about that in the beginning."

They had reached the director's bungalow, and both turned their attention to it.

"Of course, the bungalow's going to have to be done up," said Charlotte. "Nobody will want to live there after what happened."

"That'll be up to Nancy and Harvey," said Paula firmly. "I'm not doing it."

Charlotte peered closer at the building. "Does that door look open to you?"

Paula took a few steps toward it. "I think it is," she said.

Charlotte put Rupert on his leash, and the three cautiously approached the bungalow. Charlotte handed Rupert's leash to Paula, quietly opened the screen door and, with her fingertips, pushed the wooden door all the way open. She crossed the kitchen and entered the sitting room. The curtains had been opened, washing the room in a pale light, and a figure in a gray suit emerged from the bedroom.

"Hello, Nancy," said Charlotte.

"Charlotte! What are you doing here? You startled me."

"We saw the door was open, so we just came in to check. Is everything all right?"

"Yes, yes, of course it is. I was just taking a look around the place. We're going to have to decide what's to be done with it."

"Mrs. Van Dusen and I were just talking about that as we were passing."

"I suppose we'll have to spend money we haven't got fixing it up," said Nancy, her sallow face tight with annoyance. "At the very least, everything will have to be professionally cleaned and painted. That man left everything in a terrible state, not to mention what the police did. The problems he's caused us."

"Some furniture will have to be replaced too," said Charlotte, tipping her head in the direction of the sofa, now hidden under a sheet, upon which Edmund Albright's body had been found. Traces of blood on the wall behind it were still visible.

"You seemed upset by the news that the play was going to be done in the Civil War style," said Charlotte. "How are you feeling about that now?"

"What's it matter how I feel? I've got nothing to do with the theater operation. I did think, though," she said as she dropped a couple of throw cushions into a bag, "that once that awful man was gone, things would go back to normal."

"Back to normal?" asked Paula, who had entered the room with Rupert.

"Back to the way things used to be. With the plays being performed the way they should be." She glared at Charlotte, unable to risk meeting Paula's gaze. "But if it all goes to hell in a handbasket, don't look at me, and don't say you weren't warned. Still, I suppose you know what you're doing."

Chapter 25

Saturday morning, Charlotte and Rupert returned from their first walk of the day to find Ray seated at the kitchen table sipping a coffee. The morning was bright and clear, with a definite nip of autumn in the air. Charlotte slipped off her jacket and wrapped her arms around Ray while Rupert trotted off to his water bowl.

"Did you have a busy shift?" she asked. "You look tired."

"You look beautiful." Charlotte laughed. "No, really, you do. That fresh air makes your skin, oh, I don't know, but you just look lovely." Charlotte placed her cool face next to his, and he held her for a moment. He released her, then pushed a copy of the *New York Times* on the table closer to her. "You mentioned that article about Audrey Ashley is in today's paper, so I brought a copy home for you."

"Oh, that's great, thank you." Rupert walked over and stood beside her, wagging his bottom encouragingly. "Yes, Rupert," she said to him, "I haven't forgotten you." She prepared his breakfast, then poured a cup of coffee for herself, picked up the newspaper, and pulled out the arts section. "Now let's see how she did."

"What do you mean, how she did?"

"Well, is she section front or buried inside? How newsworthy is she?" She unfolded the newspaper on the table. "Oh, she will be pleased. And Maxine will be even happier, as she's the one who arranged this. She's not just Audrey's manager, she's also her sister, remember."

"Oh. Like a stage mother, you mean? Full of ambition for her talented child?"

"Yes. Full of ambition for her talented sibling."

Ray yawned and stood up. "Well, I'm off to get some sleep. I'll leave you to read in peace. Man, I hate working nights. I'll be glad when Phil gets back from vacation and I can go back to working days."

Charlotte made a little murmur of having heard him but did not look up. The article, written in Fletcher Macmillan's ingratiating style that apparently even the best newspaper editors found difficult to tame, described the Ashley family history in glowing terms, bordering on the obsequious. But to give them their due, they were exceptionally accomplished. Charlotte couldn't think of a similar family today they could be compared to. Macmillan outlined the great acting family's history: father Sir James Ashley's stature as one of the great British theater knights; mother Mary, the prolific novelist and screen writer; elder daughter Maxine's accomplishments in theater production before taking on the role of her sister's manager; and finally Audrey's childhood fame that she had sustained into her adult years.

Charlotte took a sip of tepid coffee and thought about the family dynamics. She guessed Maxine was fifteen or sixteen years older than Audrey, who had come along as one of those surprise babies born to parents who assumed their reproductive years were behind them. Audrey must have been highly prized, with the whole family lavishing her with attention and praise and, ultimately, setting aside their own career aspirations to support hers. According to the article, her career had started slowly, then came a lucky break, and finally she and her father had been cast in the same film, and although he was a serious actor of international standing, it was his little girl who commanded the spotlight. The British media went crazy for her, as only they can.

Charlotte folded the arts section of the newspaper, glanced at the headlines and scanned a few articles in the other sections, then put the paper to one side. Rupert, curled up in his basket, watched her through lazy eyes, waiting to see what would happen next. Charlotte wasn't sure herself, but something in that article bothered her. She reopened the newspaper to the story, carefully tore the paper along the centerfold, and removed the page. After folding it and setting it to one side, she called Paula Van Dusen and, an hour later, was in her office.

*

Charlotte stood at the whiteboard, a black marker in her hand, facing Paula, who was seated on the butterscotch-colored leather sofa, one arm around Coco and the other around Rupert.

WHO KILLED EDMUND ALBRIGHT? Charlotte had printed in capital letters across the board. Underneath the heading she set up two columns, titled "Suspect" and "Motive."

"Let's start at the beginning," Charlotte began. "Or rather, the end, and go over what we know. Edmund Albright went to a dinner party here at Oakland and returned home to the hotel with the rest of the party. He was seen safely to his bungalow and discovered shot to death the next morning by Audrey Ashley and me. The authorities have determined his death a likely suicide, yet we know of no reason why he would do that . . . In fact, the opposite. According to Brian Prentice, who knew him in London, Edmund was pleased to be here with our theater company and saw this opportunity as an important and useful stepping-stone in his career. We didn't see any indication that he was depressed or in a suicidal state of mind. He didn't say anything to anyone that would have indicated he was contemplating such a thing. Even his mother thought it unlikely he would commit suicide. She went so far as to write to us, to tell us so, and ask for our help. And what's more, he didn't leave a note.

"Now let's list our suspects and their motives. We'll start with Mattie."

Charlotte turned away to write on the board, then turned back to face Paula, in response to her question: "Mattie?"

"We have to include everyone," Charlotte said. "Everyone who could possibly have done it, even if we don't care for the possibility that someone we like could have been involved. And that includes Mattie."

"And her motive was . . ."

"Sexual." Paula raised her eyebrows. "I know. It seemed like he was only here five minutes but he did have his way with her, or however it happened. Mattie immediately regretted it, of course, and she felt he'd taken advantage of her."

"I should think so."

"And I'm sorry I betrayed her confidence in telling you that, but I know you won't let it go any further. But there's another reason why she might have killed Edmund. She was angry with him about casting. She wanted him to consider her for the role of Beatrice, but he explained to her that was impossible, that Audrey had been contracted for the role. Still, Mattie could have been angry enough at him over both issues to kill him."

"Now who's next?"

"Well, an obvious one would be Wade Radcliffe." Charlotte wrote his name down. "Right. With Edmund out of the way, as we've already discussed, there was a possibility he would be offered the job he wanted."

"But only a possibility," said Paula. "Would he kill another human being on the off chance of being offered the director's job?"

"He might. People kill for a variety of reasons, and one of them is that someone's got something that somebody else wants." Paula repeated her words. "Yes," said Charlotte. "Like a wife, or a large sum of money."

"Or a Maltese falcon."

"Exactly! Now who's next?"

"What about Nancy?"

"Nancy. Nothing is more important to her than the hotel. If she thought the Civil War production would lead to the hotel losing business or being associated with a performance that was ridiculed, she might have bumped off Edmund in the hope that common sense would prevail and the hotel's reputation salvaged," said Charlotte.

"Yes, and she's been through some hard financial times, so she wouldn't want the hotel's bookings to drop off to the point where she got laid off again. Another job could be hard to get at her age," said Paula. "So she had a motive. Now we have to find out if she had the opportunity."

"Well, you said she used to walk home for lunch, so she lives close enough to the hotel that she could have walked over later that night, after your dinner party, and confronted Edmund." Charlotte placed an asterisk beside her name.

"And now we come to Audrey," said Paula.

"And I think we have to include Maxine," said Charlotte, adding their names to the list. "They could have done it separately, I suppose, but it seems more likely that if one of them did it, they were both involved."

"Or maybe not," said Paula. "We'd better keep an open mind about those two."

"So what's our hypothesis?" asked Charlotte. "I've heard Ray talk about this. Sometimes the police formulate a scenario of how something might have happened and then test it with evidence. If the evidence doesn't fit, they have to change the hypothesis."

"Well, our hypothesis is that someone came to Edmund's bungalow after the dinner party, and it would have been late, after everyone was asleep. And they argued, and Edmund had found the gun that Simon left behind, and whoever the visitor was got hold of the gun and killed him with it."

"So I think we have to include Barnes here," said Charlotte. "He adored Audrey. What if he'd come back later that night and seen or heard Edmund mistreating Audrey and rushed in to protect her, saw the gun, and in a moment of craziness, grabbed it and shot Edmund?"

"Yes," said Paula. "Much as I don't like the idea, I suppose we have to include him too."

Charlotte added Barnes's name to the list and then stood back and folded her arms, and the two of them contemplated the names on the board.

"So where do we go from here?" Paula asked.

Charlotte handed her the clipping from the *New York Times*. "Did you see the story in the *Times*? Fletcher Macmillan did a good job, actually. And he told me that he had done a lot of research and had really good source material, so I'm going to ask him to lend it to me. We might find something that will point us in the right direction." She checked her watch. "Sorry. I'd best be off. We've got another dress rehearsal tonight."

"Why don't I call Fletcher Macmillan and see if I can get hold of that material? If he agrees, I can send Barnes to pick it up this evening, and we can go through it tomorrow morning. Shall we say eleven?"

"Perfect. I'm sure he'll hand it over to you without expecting a favor in return. I would have had to come up with something. He always expects a trade-off from me."

"Oh, speaking of a favor, I might be able to find out something about Nancy. She called to ask me if I knew of any work going for that niece of hers. Remember she told us she has a niece staying with her? I could talk to the niece about a job and then see if she can confirm that Nancy was at home all night when Edmund was killed. If she was, we can cross Nancy off our list."

Chapter 26

The next morning, Rupert hopped out of the back seat of the Rolls-Royce and raced around the side of the house. The front door opened, and Paula, glasses around her neck on a black cord and wearing a pale-pink sweater set with a pair of gray flannel trousers, welcomed Charlotte.

"Rupert's just gone 'round the side of the house," Charlotte said. "I expect he's looking for Ned."

"He'll be fine. Ned's out there with Coco, and he'll look after both of them. He really enjoys having them around, and when he thinks it's time for them to come in, he'll bring them 'round to the kitchen. Come on in, and let's get started."

She led the way to her office, and they seated themselves at the table.

"Did you find anything interesting?" Charlotte asked as she slipped off her jacket and hung it on the back of a chair.

"Nothing that struck me as significant," said Paula. "Fletcher's certainly accumulated a lot of material." She gestured at the table. "Books, newspaper articles off the Internet going way back, lots of family history, interviews with her parents. It's all there. I didn't realize Fletcher Macmillan did so much research."

"There was something that struck me in his article in the *Times*," said Charlotte. "He mentioned that when she was a child, Audrey was the understudy in some production or other and then caught what Fletcher described as a 'lucky break' and was moved into the leading role. Did you see anything about that anywhere?"

Paula shook her head. "No, but there might be something in here." She handed Charlotte a book on Britain's theatrical families from Fletcher's research material. Charlotte took it to the sofa and flipped it open to the section on the Ashleys, which had been marked with a yellow sticky note. Paula continued to sift through the documents on the table.

"Here it is," said Charlotte a few minutes later. "A production of *Peter Pan*. The young actress playing Wendy was injured during a dress rehearsal, and Audrey was given the role. Doesn't provide much detail, though." She looked up from the book. "But there's significance in the timing. The little girl was injured at a dress rehearsal, so it would have been Audrey in the role on opening night, when all the critics were there and the reviews were being written."

Paula got up from the table and sat beside her. "Let me see." She read the brief passage and then looked at Charlotte.

"It looks eerily like what happened to Mattie."

"I'm not sure if it means anything or not, but we'll make a note of it in case it turns out to be important. I can't see how it could, but Ray told me police always look for patterns. Things that recur. Because if something worked once, people often try it again. And again, and that's how they get caught."

Before Paula could reply, they were interrupted by a knock on the door, followed by the sound of the door opening. Rupert rushed in, with Coco chasing him. A smiling young woman entered last. She set a tray on the table with a pot of fresh coffee and two chocolate croissants.

"Fresh from Bentley's," she said. "Barnes picked them up this morning."

"Oh!" exclaimed Charlotte, writing on the whiteboard. "When I was clearing out Edmund's belongings, I found a receipt from Bentley's for two coffees and a chocolate croissant in the pocket of his jacket."

"That doesn't sound important," said Paula. "Everybody knows Bentley's has delicious pastries. You can barely get through the door on Sunday mornings."

"I think Edmund was at Bentley's with Audrey. We know she doesn't eat sweets, which is why there's just the one croissant on the receipt."

"I don't see any significance in that," said Paula. "So what if they went out for a coffee?"

Charlotte reviewed the notes on the whiteboard.

"Still, I'd like to speak to someone at Bentley's. They're probably too busy this morning."

"Later this afternoon would be better," agreed Paula. "It's the late morning rush, and then they'll be into the lunch service."

"Speaking of lunch, it's time I was heading home. Ray's working nights, and he'll be up soon. We don't see all that much of each other during the week, so it'd be nice to spend a bit of time together this afternoon."

"Does he know about this?" Paula gestured at the whiteboard.

"No. I've urged him to ask the state police to take another look at the case, but he says they won't do that just because somebody like me disagrees with their findings or says it doesn't feel right. He said if new evidence turned up, that would be different."

"Well, maybe we can find something that would convince them to take another look."

"Maybe we can. About Bentley's—second thought. Would you be free to meet there for coffee tomorrow morning about eleven? That's the time stamp on the receipt, so we if we go then, there's a chance we could talk to the same server who looked after Edmund and Audrey, if that's who he was with."

"Let me check." Paula removed the elastic band from her bulging engagement diary and flipped a page. "Tomorrow's fine." She made a note in the planner. "Do you think we accomplished anything this morning?"

"I think so," Charlotte replied slowly. "Lots to think about, but it all seems disorganized up here." She tapped her temple. "But here"—she pointed at the whiteboard—"it helps to lay it all out in a visual way. And hopefully, if we ask the right questions, we'll get a clearer picture of what happened."

As Charlotte gathered up her belongings and clipped Rupert on his leash, Paula remarked, "I'm expecting Belinda this afternoon." Belinda, Paula's only child, had been about to marry a high-flying Manhattan real estate agent in June when the wedding had to be suddenly postponed. The couple then set a Christmas date, but for several reasons, Belinda had decided to call that one off too.

"I'm afraid to ask," said Charlotte.

"Oh, it's off again," said Paula cheerfully. "And let's hope it stays off."

*

Ray was seated at the kitchen table drinking coffee when Charlotte and Rupert returned. His hair was still wet and tousled from the shower, and he was dressed in his uniform.

"Why are you dressed?" Charlotte asked over her shoulder as she changed the water in Rupert's water bowl. "Are you going in early? I was looking forward to us spending some time together this afternoon. We need to talk about what we're going to do about the trip to England."

"I'm not going in for a while. We can talk about that. In fact, I'd love to talk about that."

Charlotte slid into the seat beside him and reached for his hand. "We should go. I'll talk to Wade tomorrow and let him know we're going. I'm not going to ask if it's okay. I'm entitled to time off and I'm going to take it. Aaron can keep a lid on things here."

Ray put his arm around her. "Tell me what dates you want and I'll book the flight."

"I'll let you know later today." She pulled back and gave him a luminous smile.

"Happy?"

"Very. But I'd be a bit happier if you had the rest of the day off and we could go somewhere."

"Phil's due back in a few days and the shifts will be back to normal," he reassured her. "I can't wait. We were really busy last night. Picked up an underage driver speeding in a car packed with teenagers. They'd all been drinking. The driver's facing some really serious charges." He drained the last of his coffee. "I almost feel sorry for people who wake up in a police cell with a massive hangover, wondering how the hell they got into this mess and how they're going to get out of it. And of course, in this case, we've got some very upset parents to deal with."

Charlotte didn't hear the last couple of sentences. Her gaze shifted away from Ray to the window. She stared at the river, unseeing, while she tried to make sense of what he'd just said. Something had rung a little bell in the back of her mind. *Serious Charges.*

Chapter 27

Warm air, fragrant with the aroma of freshly ground coffee, greeted Charlotte as she entered Bentley's Bistro. The busy breakfast period, when people dashed in to grab a coffee and bagel or muffin, was over, and lunch service had not yet begun. Just a few tables were occupied, including one beside the window where Paula Van Dusen waited for her.

Paula gave her a welcoming smile as Charlotte slid into the seat opposite her.

"I haven't been here in ages," said Paula. "It looks much better now. It used to be so dark and dreary."

They chatted for a couple of minutes until their server arrived. Dressed in black trousers with a white shirt, he appeared to be in his early twenties.

"A latte for me, please," said Paula.

"I'll have the same," said Charlotte. "Oh, and have you got any chocolate croissants? We'll have one to share, if you've got any."

"We do," said the server. As he tapped their order into his tablet, Charlotte withdrew two theater publicity photographs from her bag—one of Edmund Albright and the other of Audrey Ashley—and laid them on the table. The server leaned forward to take a closer look at them. "Are they friends of yours, if you don't mind me asking?"

"Not exactly friends, no," said Charlotte. "I work with them. At least, I work with her." She tapped the photo of Audrey. "Sadly, this man died recently."

"No way!" said the waiter. "They were in here recently. They both had English accents, which is a bit unusual. That's why I remembered them. I served them myself."

"Did you?" said Charlotte. "If you've got a minute, we'd like to know what you can remember about them."

He checked his tablet. "I'll be right back. Got a few orders ready."

He returned a few minutes later and placed two lattes, a chocolate croissant, and an extra plate on the table.

"They were in here recently," he repeated. "Sat over there." He gestured vaguely toward the rear of the dining room. "I remember them because they were whisper-arguing. That's what I call it when people argue in here, but they keep their voices down. But you can tell from the body language that they're having a disagreement. I came to take their order, but they just ignored me, like I wasn't there. So I waited, like I'm supposed to. It happens all the time. People think waitstaff are invisible and just ignore us."

Paula and Charlotte exchanged a sharp, hopeful look.

"And can you tell us what they were saying?" Charlotte asked as she cut the croissant in two and placed half on the extra plate and handed it to Paula.

"I don't remember the exact words, but he said something like, 'I wonder what poor little Gillian's parents would have to say about that, not to mention the police,' and she's like in a hissy fit and telling him he's got it all wrong and it was an accident. But now that I think about it, she looked scared." His eyes met those of the woman glaring at him from behind the counter. "I'd better go. Getting the stink eye from the boss."

"You've been really helpful," said Charlotte. "Sorry we took up so much of your time. Thank you."

"No problem." With a professional smile, he glided away to see to the needs of the customers at a neighboring table.

"Well," said Paula. "And what do we make of that?" She took a dainty bite of her croissant.

"We need to find out who poor little Gillian is and what happened to her."

"I've seen that name," said Paula. "I'm pretty sure it's mentioned in one of the articles in that pile of clippings Fletcher Macmillan sent over. I can't remember the last name though. Gillian . . . something?"

Charlotte took out her phone, pulled up Google, and typed in "Audrey Ashley Gillian." A moment later, a list of possible matches appeared, and she clicked on one. "Gillian Pritchard?"

"That sounds familiar," said Paula.

Charlotte scanned a newspaper story. "Oh, now, this is interesting. It says here Gillian Pritchard was playing Wendy in a Christmas pantomime version of *Peter Pan* when she was seriously injured in what was classified as an industrial accident at the theater, and her understudy took over." She peered at Paula. "You can guess who her understudy was."

"Young Miss Audrey Ashley."

"The very same. This is the big career break Fletcher mentioned in his story. Audrey was the understudy for the Wendy role, and when the girl playing Wendy was unable to perform, Audrey took over. Let's see what else it says." She took a sip of coffee and continued reading. "Oh, no!"

"What?"

"Gillian died a few months later. She was in hospital and never recovered from her injuries."

"What on earth happened?"

"A counterweight fell off a catwalk during a dress rehearsal and hit her. She never recovered consciousness.

"And even though the accident happened more than thirty years ago, there would have been strict safety measures in place, especially in a production like that with performers in harnesses on wires for the flying scenes. Which is probably what the counterweights were for.

"There would have been an investigation into the accident, and another inquest after Gillian died. The story was in all the newspapers at the time, and it would certainly have been much talked about in theater circles."

"So what are you getting at?" Paula said. "Do you think Audrey had something to do with what happened to poor Gillian?" asked Paula. "Is that likely? She was only, what, twelve or thirteen years old at the time."

"No, not Audrey," Charlotte replied, "but Maxine is more than ambitious enough for the two of them. And she would have been twenty-five or so. Also, having grown up in a theatrical family and worked in theater production, she would have known her way around a theater, having spent a lot of time there. She could probably go into any backstage area of the theater she liked without anyone taking any notice of her. She might have waited for her chance, climbed up onto the catwalk, and tossed a weight over the side."

"So where does this leave us? What does it mean? Where do we go from here?" Paula asked.

Charlotte considered her answer before replying.

"I'm not sure where this gets us. Anyway, something that Ray said reminded me that the play that Audrey appeared in that Edmund directed was called *Serious Charges*. I've ordered a copy of it from the Drama Book

Shop." She checked her watch and groaned slightly. "I'd better be thinking about getting to work. We've got a performance this afternoon."

"Before we go, I've got something to tell you. I spoke to Nancy's niece last night. It turns out Sonja Harrison's looking for a personal assistant, so I've put them in touch. I steered the conversation around to how she likes living with her aunt and found a way to ask her about Nancy. The thing is, the niece says Nancy arrived home from the dinner party and didn't go out again that night."

"But how would she know?" asked Charlotte. "The niece could have been asleep, Nancy slips out, kills Edmund, and returns home."

"Well, the niece said she couldn't get to sleep, so she went downstairs about one o'clock and made some toast, which burned and set off the smoke alarm. Nancy came rushing downstairs in her dressing gown, obviously just woken up."

Charlotte nodded. "We can rule Nancy out, then."

"I think we can. And now, how about we run you home," said Paula, standing up and pulling on a light-blue wool coat. "This has been a most stimulating conversation. Thought provoking. Really makes you think."

"It certainly does," said Charlotte as they left the bistro and walked up the street to where Barnes had parked the car. "It's got me thinking about what happened to Mattie during the dress rehearsal. Is there a connection to what happened to Gillian? I read something once that really stayed with me," she said slowly, "and I wonder if it applies here."

Paula raised an eyebrow. "What's that?"

"'The explanation for a murder often lies in a previous murder.'"

Chapter 28

Three days later, Aaron arrived in the office holding a small parcel, which he held out to Charlotte.

"This just came for you."

She thanked him, opened the padded envelope, and pulled out the *Serious Charges* script. As she thumbed through a few pages, she felt Aaron's eyes on her and looked up to see him watching her.

"What is it?" she asked.

"Are you going to read that now?"

"Yes, I am. Why? Do you need me for something?"

"No. Just wondering if you remembered that it's opening night tonight, that's all. Can I get you a cup of tea or anything?"

"No thanks, because on second thought, since you've done such a wonderful job of getting everything ready for the opening, I'm going to take this home and read it there.

I'll just be an hour or so, and you can always ring me if you need me."

She tucked the little book in her bag and, a few minutes later, let herself into the bungalow. Rupert greeted her from his basket in the kitchen. She went through to the sitting room, stretched out on the sofa, and opened the book. As she was rearranging the cushions under her head, Rupert joined her, climbed up onto the sofa, and snuggled in. She draped her arm lightly around him and began to read.

An hour and a half later, Charlotte finished the script and closed the book. She knew how the killer had done it—how they'd shot Edmund and made it look like suicide using a simple technique to trick the police forensics teams.

What Charlotte didn't know was who did it.

"Come on, Rupert, let's get you out, and then I have to get back to work. Aaron's not best pleased with me today."

The morning had started out fair, but menacing clouds now hung over the mountaintops, threatening rain. The fair days of fall had crossed into the cold and blustery days that spoke of the promise of the coming winter. The path to the hotel was littered with dry, brittle leaves that crackled underfoot as she walked to the hotel's back entrance.

"Everything all right?" she asked Aaron as she entered her office.

He hung a man's costume on an almost full garment rack before replying. "No problems. I've just got to deliver these to the dressing rooms, and then I'm going for lunch.

I'll be getting the props and everything ready backstage this afternoon. Will Ray be doing the prompts tonight?"

"Yes, he will. And what about the after party? Did Nancy ask for your help with that?"

"She ordered all the food and drinks, and the cafeteria people are going to set everything up."

Charlotte consulted the opening-night list. "And presentation flowers for the leading lady?"

"Mrs. Van Dusen is picking them up and bringing them."

"Good. Well done, Aaron. Sounds as if we're in good shape. Oh, and how's Mattie doing?"

"She's fine. She can walk okay, but she might have a little trouble with the dance at the end."

"Well, maybe she won't be quite as sprightly as usual, but she'll give it her best, that's for sure. And I'm sure the cast is filled with all the usual opening-night jitters, but they'll do us proud. They always do."

*

Surprisingly, for a production that had got off to such a rocky start and been beset with so many problems, the opening-night performance went well. Everyone remembered their lines, entrances and exits were flawless, and Charlotte was delighted that no one tore a costume or split a seam. Maxine, who was dressing Audrey, watched parts of the play from a quiet spot backstage. She spoke to no one, kept out of the way, and scurried back and forth to

Audrey's dressing room to be available when Audrey came offstage.

As the play ended, the curtains swished shut, and the cast took their places onstage for the first curtain call. The curtain opened, and they all joined hands, stepped forward, and bowed. The actors cast in minor roles disappeared into the wings and headed for their dressing rooms while the main characters once again acknowledged the applause. All the actors except Audrey Ashley then exited the stage, leaving her to prepare for her spotlight moment. On her signal, the curtains swung open one last time. Audrey dropped a deep, elegant curtsy, balancing gracefully as she bowed her head and extended her left arm to the audience in an embracing gesture. She held the pose, basking in the applause. As she rose, Paula Van Dusen crossed the stage and gently placed a showstopper cellophane-and-ribbon-wrapped bouquet of ruby-red roses, creamy-white lilies, and purple lisianthus in Audrey's outstretched arms. And then, with perfect timing, Aaron closed the curtain at the precise moment the applause started to die down, and Maxine rushed onstage to escort Audrey to her dressing room. Audrey thrust the flowers into her hands and, with Maxine trailing behind her, headed for her dressing room. No one spoke to her, but this was not unusual, as many stage performers, actors, and musicians do not like to be approached or spoken to on their way on or off stage.

Charlotte watched them go and then glanced at Paula, who had joined her.

"I think I know how Edmund was murdered," Charlotte whispered and then added, before Paula could reply, "I've got to take care of the costumes now, but I'll tell you my theory later."

"Have you told Ray?" Paula asked.

"No, I haven't. I just worked it out this morning and he was at work all day. I want to put everything together and make sure I've got all the bits and pieces in place before I tell him."

"Tell me what?" asked Ray, who had watched the curtain calls from his prompt desk, then spent a few minutes talking to audience members before they left the theater.

"Sorry, got to go," said Charlotte. "Have to check in the costumes and get items ready for the laundry." Dressed in a black turtleneck sweater and black trousers, she faded into the black wing curtains that led to the backstage area, leaving a puzzled Ray in her wake.

"Tell me what?" Ray repeated.

"Oh," said Paula. "Well, I think she's planning a little surprise for you. I'm not sure of the details, though. Probably best if she tells you herself." She looked wildly around the now empty area. "I think I'd better get myself to the rehearsal room and make sure everything's set up for the after party."

"Maybe it's about the trip we're planning to the UK," mused Ray.

Chapter 29

"I should circulate," Paula remarked to Charlotte. "I need to congratulate the cast on behalf of the board, and then we can talk over dinner."

A section of the hotel's main restaurant had been set up for the opening-night after party. Soft lighting, white table-cloths on round tables graced with floral centerpieces, and a lavish candlelit buffet created an atmosphere of welcome hospitality.

"This is the nicest after party we've ever had," said Charlotte, admiring the setup. "Usually it's cheese and crackers and a glass of cheap wine in the rehearsal room. And that's if we're lucky."

"After all the money the theater generates for Harvey Jacobs and everything you've been through getting this production up and running, I told him it was the least he could do for the company," Paula said. "Still, you know what he's like. It wasn't easy getting him to agree to put on a spread like this. He doesn't understand that money spent on hospitality is usually money well spent. And he's in the hospitality business! Oh, look out! Fletcher Macmillan's headed our way. Shall I talk to him or will you?"

"Oh, I'm sure it's you he wants to speak to. And we have to be nice to him, because those research documents he loaned us were really useful."

"Well, we'll be nice to him for a little while, anyway."

Paula, wearing a tailored burgundy-colored evening suit that was neither too dressy nor too casual for the occasion, glided off to speak to Fletcher just as Charlotte's phone rang. She turned her back on the room and answered it. Ray, who had returned home to see to Rupert, had received a call from the on-duty police officer that there'd been a serious road traffic accident and all officers were needed to assist. Ray assured her that he'd try to make it back to the party but couldn't make any promises.

Charlotte was mildly disappointed but not surprised. Living with a police officer meant unpredictable hours, and she understood and accepted that. As much as he sometimes wanted to do something, there were times when the job just had to come first.

Actors—their makeup creamed and tissued off and changed into party clothes—accompanied by crew members, trickled, then poured into the restaurant. Everyone was relieved and happy that the first performance of this unusual season was behind them. Paula circled the room, pausing to stop and chat with everyone. She beamed at

Mattie, shook hands with Audrey, and thanked and congratulated Wade. Finally satisfied that she'd spoken to everyone, she scooped up two glasses of wine and headed in Charlotte's direction.

"Let's sit." She pointed to a table at the end of the buffet, set back a little from the others, with a reserved sign on it. "I asked them to save this table for me. We should be able to talk here without being overheard. But first, let's get our food. I'm starving, and you must be too."

When they were seated, Paula unfolded a napkin onto her lap and picked up her wine glass. "Tell me," she said.

Charlotte began. "Here's what I think happened. Remember we talked about Gillian Pritchard and the accident in the theater?" Paula took a sip of wine and nodded. "Right, well, the scrap of conversation that the server at Bentley's Bistro overheard suggests that either Edmund knew or suspected that Gillian had been deliberately hurt so Audrey, as the understudy, could take over the Wendy role. Unfortunately, this has happened before in the theater, when desperately ambitious people do something terrible to get what they want. I believe the person who dropped the weight off the catwalk was Maxine. And when Edmund threatened to use this knowledge to gain something to his advantage from Audrey, she realized that the only way she could stop him would be to kill him. Not only did she have her career to think of—she's been cast in a big period drama that's going to be very popular—but she thinks she's in with a chance to be named as a dame in the New Year's Honours list."

"What's that mean?"

"In the UK, a damehood is awarded to women like a knighthood is to men. It's a big deal, and believe me, she wants it. Very badly."

"So you think Audrey killed Edmund."

"I think it's a real possibility, and it makes sense. I think she went 'round to see him after your dinner party. To talk to him. What about, I don't know. Probably not the Civil War version of the play, because that was settled at your dinner party, but maybe about whatever it was that he wanted from her. He made a pot of tea, they drank it, and at some point, she found the gun and realized she could use it to kill him and make it look like suicide. Job done and problem solved."

Paula frowned. "Really?"

Charlotte broke a piece off a bread roll and leaned forward as she buttered it.

"I know what you're thinking," she said. "You're wondering how Audrey could kill him and make it look like suicide. And you're right. It's really hard to get past the police forensics testing. They'd check for gunpowder residue on his hand. But she knew how to do this, because she did it in a play called *Serious Charges*, which she starred in and Edmund directed. And that's the really awful part of all this. When poor Edmund was sat on the sofa, Audrey joined him there, sat close to him, and then, because he directed the play, for an awful few seconds, he would have known what was coming."

Paula put down her fork. "You mean he knew she was going to kill him?"

Charlotte nodded. "He knew. You see, she had a plastic bag over her hand when she fired the gun. After she'd fired it, she peeled the bag off her hand and carefully placed it over his hand, then gently rubbed it so the gunpowder residue would transfer from the bag onto his hand. She didn't need to worry about there being any residue on her own hand because it was unlikely that the police would test her for it, and if they ever did, by the time they got around to it, any traces would be washed away and worn off. And she knew from the play where to sit beside him and how to position the gun so when she pulled the trigger, the bullet angle would look like suicide."

Paula mulled this over. "But why would he just sit there and let her point a gun at his head? Wouldn't he have jumped up, tried to escape, or put up a fight?"

"Not if she was holding the gun to one side, like this," Charlotte stood up to demonstrate, holding her right hand slightly behind her back, then sliding into the chair beside Paula's. She placed her left hand on Paula's upper arm, leaned into her, and suddenly raised her right hand to Paula's temple. "Like that." Paula turned her head slightly toward Charlotte and found herself looking into the cold, hard eyes of Maxine, several tables away. Maxine shifted slightly in her seat and said something to Audrey.

"Don't look now, but Maxine just saw what you did. I hope it doesn't mean anything to her. Do you think she knows?"

"Knows what Audrey did? Oh, yes, she knows. Audrey couldn't possibly have killed someone and not told Maxine. Audrey would have called her right after it happened, don't you think? And not only that, it's possible that Maxine helped with the cleanup. I mean, wouldn't you phone someone and ask for help?"

"Yes," said Paula. "After everything you've just told me, I'd probably call you. On second thought, maybe not. You'd feel you had to tell Ray. Speaking of which, when are you going to tell him all this? He knows you're up to something."

"I'd like to tell him tonight, but I don't have any proof or evidence, or anything to support my theory, and I need something substantial if he's to take this seriously."

*

The theater people had finished their meals and, after a few encouraging and congratulatory words from their director, were beginning to file out of the restaurant. It was late, they were tired, and the postperformance adrenaline that had surged through their bodies had worn off. Now they were well fed and happy, but exhausted.

Maxine and Audrey remained in their seats until the room had cleared, then sauntered over to Paula and Charlotte's table.

"Not ready to leave yet?" Maxine asked pleasantly.

"We were just thinking about it," replied Paula.

"Well, thank you for a lovely party," said Audrey. "Everyone enjoyed it."

"I'm glad to hear that," said Paula. "You deserved it."

"Too bad Edmund didn't live to enjoy seeing his version of the play on its opening night," Charlotte said to Audrey. "Do you think the performance would have pleased him? Would it have been everything he'd imagined?"

"I really have no idea," replied Audrey, frost forming on every word. "And now, if you'll excuse me, I'm tired and off to my bed."

Maxine reached out to support Audrey, and the two walked toward the door. Just as they reached it, Maxine turned around and gave the two women a look of such venomous hatred that Paula started.

"We have to do something tonight," she said. "My stomach is positively churning from that look she gave us."

"Let me think," Charlotte said. "There must be something we've overlooked."

Paula picked up her purse. "I don't think we should stay here alone," she said. "What if they come back? We need to get where there are other people, and we need to stay together. Let's go to the lobby, and we can wait for Barnes there."

"Wait!" cried Charlotte. "Where is he?" She looked wildly at Paula, who returned her look with one of confusion.

"Who? Where's who?"

"Barnes! We should have asked Barnes!"

Chapter 30

"Barnes, people sometimes see things that they don't recognize as being important at the time. Now we know you dropped off some flowers for Audrey Ashley at the star bungalow on the night Edmund Albright died, but don't worry. We're not here to talk about that. What we want to know is, What time were you there?"

"I don't know. It was after midnight but not yet one o'clock. Sometime in there."

"And did you see or hear anything?"

"Like what? I didn't hear a gunshot, if that's what you're asking."

"No, I didn't think you would have," said Charlotte, "because he was very likely dead before you got there. Now, this is important, so please think carefully. Did you see anyone in the grounds?"

"Well, yes, I think I did. At least, I'm pretty sure it was that night, because that was the last night I dropped off the flowers." He could not bring himself to meet either of their eyes.

"Who did you see, Barnes?" Seated beside each other on a dark-brown sofa in the hotel lobby, Charlotte and Paula waited for him to respond. When Paula seemed about to prompt him, Charlotte touched her lightly on the arm, pinched her lips together, and gave a light shake of her head.

"I saw her."

"Who, Barnes? Who did you see?"

"Why, Miss Ashley, of course. She came out of the director's bungalow and ran toward her own house."

"And where were you?"

"I was, well, let's just say I was nearby." *He can't bring himself to utter the undignified words "I was hiding in the bushes,"* thought Charlotte.

"And why didn't you tell the police what you saw?" Paula asked. "You should have come forward, Barnes. You know that."

"How could I? They'd have wanted to know what I was doing there at that time of night. And anyway, this fellow committed suicide, didn't he? So what would be the point?"

Charlotte sighed. "Well, the police are going to want to talk to you now, I'm sure. Although seeing Audrey Ashley come out of the director's bungalow doesn't mean she killed him."

"Killed him!" said Barnes.

"Yes," said Paula. "That's what this is all about. That's why we need you to tell the police exactly what you saw."

"It's time to call Ray," said Charlotte.

*

The door into the hotel lobby opened and Ray entered, with Audrey on one side and Maxine on the other.

"It's a little unorthodox, I know," he said, "but Audrey and Maxine wanted to hear what Charlotte has to say, so I agreed to arrange a meeting."

"You've got it all wrong," Maxine shouted. "Audrey didn't kill Edmund. I did."

"No, Maxine," said Charlotte. "You didn't. And while it's natural for you to want to protect Audrey, I'm afraid this time you can't. You didn't kill Edmund Albright."

When Maxine started to protest, Charlotte held up her hand.

"It's no use. But don't worry, Maxine. There's enough murder to go around. I'm sure you didn't intend for Gillian Pritchard to die, but you killed her so Audrey could take over the lead female role of Wendy in the production of *Peter Pan*, a role that you rightly realized would catapult her to stardom. There was no shortage of love in the Ashley family. Everyone adored little Audrey, and when her acting talents began to emerge, the whole family worked together to give her every chance of success. There was never any doubt that she was going to be a star. And Maxine, you made sure that the opportunity presented itself, but sadly, at Gillian's expense."

Audrey raised horrified eyes to her sister. "Is this true?" she croaked.

Charlotte then described how Audrey had killed Edmund Albright, making it look like a suicide. Audrey clung to her sister as her eyes filled with tears, and her body shook with huge sobs. "It's not true! I didn't do it! I was there, that's true, but he was alive when I left him! I swear he was."

Ray phoned for backup.

Chapter 31

With Audrey detained overnight for questioning, Charlotte thought she'd feel some sense of satisfaction. But she didn't. *I know what acting looks like*, she thought. *I see it every day.* But when Audrey protested that she didn't kill Edmund, Charlotte didn't think she wasn't acting. The truth was in her eyes. And when she was led away, shaking and crying, her terror seemed genuine.

Did I get it wrong? Charlotte thought. *But everything fit together so perfectly. It had to have happened that way.*

Charlotte wasn't the only one plagued with doubt. Mattie, preparing to step into the leading role of Beatrice at the next performance, was nervous and unsure about the part and unhappy about the way she'd landed it. Her fidgeting and pacing during a hastily arranged costume fitting finally got the better of Charlotte.

"Mattie! Stand still. I can't do this when you're all over the place."

"Sorry. It's just that I thought I wanted this, and now I realize I don't. I was happier as Hero. The part fit me better."

"I guess it's a reminder we should all be careful what we wish for," Charlotte said.

Charlotte went home as soon as the matinee performance was under way. Uneasy and unsettled, she fetched Rupert, and the two set off on a walk. The leaves on the trees were turning now, streaks of autumn color cutting orange, yellow, and red swathes through the green trees that covered the sides of the nearby mountains.

As they passed the star bungalow, a curtain moved to one side, and a moment later, Maxine came tearing out. Her gray hair was wild and uncombed, and she clutched a black cardigan to her chest as she hurried after Charlotte.

"You've got to help her," she cried, the desperate words tumbling out in an anguished torrent. "There's been a terrible mistake. Please, see what you can do. Talk to the police. Audrey didn't do it. He was alive when she left him."

"I'd like to help, but I don't know what I can do," Charlotte said. "The police are looking into it, and if Audrey didn't do it, I'm sure they'll come to that conclusion." Maxine turned away and ran back into the bungalow, her slippered feet sliding on the path.

Deeply troubled, Charlotte returned home. After spending some time listlessly reading, tidying up, and always circling back to the disturbing image of Maxine begging for her help, she put the kettle on. Just as she poured a cup of tea, a knock on the door startled her.

She opened it to find Aaron with a pair of gray trousers draped over his arm, the brown leather suspenders attached to them almost touching the ground.

"I'm really sorry to bother you with this," he said, "but I agreed to drive my aunt to an appointment in Saugerties." He held the trousers a little closer to Charlotte.

"Don John split the seam open. I'm really hoping that you can fix them in time for tonight's performance. It's not a big job, and I would have done it, but because it's a rented costume, I thought it best if you take care of it."

Charlotte reached out her arms. "Give them here. I was rather looking for something to do this afternoon. Off you go."

She examined the seam and, deciding it was a relatively straightforward job, left with Rupert for the hotel. Hand sewing she occasionally did at home, but for this, she needed the machine in her workroom.

A few minutes later, she let herself into her office, removed the cover from the sewing machine and, taking the trousers with her, went in search of gray thread. She held a couple of spools up to the fabric, chose the best match, and threaded the machine.

She turned the trousers inside out and quickly and smoothly repaired the torn seam. She needed to press them before returning them to the actor, so she plugged in the iron and, while she waited for it to heat, dampened a pressing cloth in the kitchenette. When the iron was hot, she spread the seam, laid the damp cloth carefully over it, and held the iron to it. A cloud of fragrant steam rose from the ironing board as she moved the iron gently back and forth.

She tipped the iron onto its heel rest, lifted the warm cloth, and examined the repaired seam. *That'll do*, she thought.

As she turned the trousers inside out and draped them over the back of a chair, she thought how clever the idea had been to have this character, Don John, play a soldier from the opposing army. Although he wasn't in the same league of villains as, say, Iago, Don John was nevertheless a pretty unlikeable guy. And having the two brothers, Don Pedro and Don John, serve on two opposing armies had added to the conflict between the two characters . . . A sudden, imperative question interrupted her thinking. Whose idea had it been to have this character dress as a soldier from the South?

It was Wade's, wasn't it? She walked to her desk and checked through the book in which she took notes during her meetings with directors. She flipped backward through the book until she found what she was looking for. Yes, dated at the top and then . . . One man's gray Southern uniform . . . others in Union blue.

But she'd had a sense in the meeting that the idea wasn't new. She must have heard it before. Where? When?

She pushed her chair back from her desk, tipped her head back, and gazed at the ceiling. The idea of having one

Southern soldier hadn't been Wade's, it had to have been Edmund's. She reached for her phone.

"Paula, that idea of having one soldier in *Much Ado* wear gray—was it Edmund's?"

She listened for a moment and then ended the call. Yes, Paula had confirmed. It was Edmund's idea. At the dinner party. Edmund suggested it right after Paula announced that the board was in favor of the Civil War production. Didn't he say something like "I've just had this great idea . . ." Just had . . .

Could Edmund and Wade both have had the same idea? Unlikely. What was it Wade had said at his first rehearsal? "I liked the idea of Don Pedro fighting on the North side and Don John for the South. That would instantly explain their estrangement to the audience. They'd understand immediately."

He *liked* the idea. Not that it was his idea, but he liked the idea. Someone else's idea. Charlotte's mind was in full flow now. Hadn't Wade also said that he hadn't discussed the play with Edmund?

With a rising sense of excitement, Charlotte considered the implication of this information. He must have discussed it with Edmund and that's where he got the idea for the North and South costuming.

Again, she reached for her phone and called Fletcher Macmillan, reporter for the *Hudson Valley Echo*. His phone went to voice mail, so she left a message asking him to ring her back at the office to confirm that Wade Radcliffe had said during the brief question-and-answer session in the theater that he had not discussed the play with Edmund Albright. Hopefully, Fletcher had written that down in his notebook.

She laid out all the pieces in her mind and carefully examined each one. Crucially, Edmund had said at the dinner party that he'd just had a great idea . . . and by next morning, he was dead. So Wade must have spoken to Edmund after the dinner party, and Audrey had insisted that Edmund was alive when she left his bungalow. Charlotte now believed that he was.

So Wade had killed him. But how did he know how to make the killing look like a suicide?

With a loud and final clang, the last piece of the puzzle fell into place.

He hadn't been in the play, *Serious Charges*, as Audrey had, but although he hadn't specified what play she'd been "wonderful" in, Charlotte had no doubt he'd seen her performance in that play in England.

Charlotte reached for her old-fashioned desk telephone and called Ray at work. Again the call went to voice mail and, frustrated, again she left a message. "It wasn't Audrey," she said. "I got the how right, but not the who. It was . . ." A finger jabbed the plunger on the phone, and the line went dead.

Chapter 32

Charlotte spun in her seat to see Wade Radcliffe towering over her. She tried to stand but he pushed her by the shoulder back into the seat. "Stay where you are," he snarled.

Charlotte glanced toward the open door. "Don't even think about it," Wade said. "There's no one out there. There's no one to help you." Her mind raced to thoughts of Ray. "And never mind your policeman boyfriend. By the time he gets here, it'll be too late."

I've got to keep him talking, Charlotte thought. *If I can just keep him talking for a few minutes.*

"How did you get the gun, Wade?" she croaked through dry lips.

"Edmund had found it hidden in the back of a drawer and left it out for anyone to see." He cackled. "Or use. Oh, it was so easy. We had a nice little chat about the play, exchanged a few ideas, and then, well, he had to go."

"Why, Wade? Why did he have to go?"

"Because I wanted the job. It was mine. I deserved it. I've spent a lifetime working in the theater, building a reputation, and then he comes along and the job is just handed to him on the whim of an English actress." He frowned. "Do you have any idea how embarrassing that was for me? Having to tell people that I didn't get the job? And they're all thinking, 'Oh, that's because he's too old.'"

"So you killed him."

"I didn't intend to. I just went over there to talk to him. To ask him if he'd bow out and return to England. He didn't need the work. I did. All he had to do was leave. But you know what he did?"

"No, Wade. What did he do?"

"He laughed. And then he told me all about his Civil War version, and you know what? I thought it was a great idea."

"You did?"

"Of course I did. But I had to pretend I didn't like it because it was his idea. And then I could be seen to come around gradually to the idea."

"So the night you went to see him, why did you go so late?"

"I knew he'd be at Paula Van Dusen's dinner party, so I . . ."

"How did you know?"

"Roger Harrison. I've known Roger for years. Ran into him at the drugstore and he mentioned Paula Van Dusen was hosting a dinner for a few theater board members and the leading lady and director." He practically spat out the

last word in the sentence. "I should have been at that dinner. That was my seat at the table."

"So you planned to talk to him afterward? Why so late?"

"It wouldn't have been that late, except Audrey got to him
before me. I had to wait around until she left, and then I went
to see him. Knocked on his door and the fool let me in. By
then, he was tired, but I persuaded him to talk to me. Said it
wouldn't take long. And you know what? It didn't!"

"Why did you wait around? Why couldn't you have
come back to talk to him during the day?"

"Because I couldn't show my face around here in broad
daylight. After the humiliation of being turned down for the
director's job?" His face twisted into a contorted mask of
anger. Charlotte's heart beat faster as she placed her hands on
the arm of her chair and tried to rise. Her knees had turned to
jelly, and she found herself unable to stand. As she sank bank
into the chair, Wade's outstretched hands reached for her neck.
She groped behind her on her desk, scrabbling to find and
pick up whatever she could reach. Her fingers closed around
the metal box that held the index cards on which she wrote the
actors' names, their characters, and costuming notes. As she
raised the box above Wade's head, determined to hit him with
it as hard as she could, the lid flew open and cards flew out.

As they fluttered to the floor, the door opened and two
men entered. Fletcher Macmillan, carrying his notebook,
looked at the scene in astonishment as the other man, the
actor playing Don John, said, "Oh, sorry. I guess you're busy.
I don't mean to bother you, but I just came to see if my pants
are ready."

Chapter 33

"I can't believe we're really going to England tonight!" Charlotte said two weeks later as she zippered her suitcase. "I miss Rupert already. I hope he'll be okay while I'm away."

"He'll be fine," said Ray. "Ned's taken a great shine to him, and Rupert'll spend the next three weeks helping him in the garden. He'll have a wonderful holiday, and by the time we come home, he'll be an expert on how to get your garden ready for winter."

Ray took her suitcase, and he and Charlotte left the bungalow and walked to the parking area, where Barnes was waiting for them.

As Ray lifted the bags into the trunk, the hotel door opened and Aaron rushed out.

"You weren't going to leave without saying good-bye, were you?" he asked Charlotte.

"We already said good-bye this morning and then again this afternoon," she laughed.

Aaron reached out to hug her. "I'll miss you." He stepped back and scanned her face. "You are coming back, aren't you?"

"Oh, don't be such a numpty! Of course I'm coming back. And if you have any questions or need me for anything, just text. But you'll be fine. Everything's going to go smoothly from now on. Everything that could possibly go wrong already has."

Aaron shook hands with Ray and then stepped back.

"Really nice of Paula to ask Barnes to drive us to the airport," Ray said as they climbed into the Rolls-Royce.

After one last wave good-bye to Aaron, they settled back into the comfortable seats, holding hands, speaking little. Charlotte gazed out the window, thinking that by the time they returned home, the trees would have shed their leaves, and winter would be just around the corner.

When they reached their destination, Barnes stood to one side as Ray lifted the suitcases out of the trunk, and a moment later, the terminal doors swished open and they entered the building.

Charlotte stood to one side watching the crowds while Ray printed out their boarding passes at the kiosk. They dropped off their bags and proceeded through security and then to their departure gate. At the gate, they stopped in front of a restaurant, and Ray asked Charlotte if she felt like a drink.

"I don't think so. My stomach is a little"—she made a swirling motion with her hand in front of her abdomen—"a little queasy. To be honest, I don't like flying."

"A cup of tea, then?" Ray suggested.

"No, I think I'll just sit here quietly and wait. But you get something if you want."

"I'll get a coffee in a few minutes. Maybe by then you'll have changed your mind and be ready for something." He sat beside her and crossed his legs. "I'm glad everything worked out so you can enjoy our time in England without worrying about what's going on at the theater. It was good that Paula was able to persuade Brian to come back and that he feels well enough to take it on."

"I couldn't stop laughing when I saw the new posters." Charlotte waved her hand in a small arc. "'Back by popular demand! Brian Prentice as guest director.' Oh, how he loves that. And we've even told him if he behaves himself, he can play the part of Leonato every now and then."

"I was sure Audrey would go back to England as soon as she was released."

"I thought that too. What a surprise when she decided to stay on. But 'helping police with their inquiries,' as we say in the UK, got her more publicity than she ever dreamed of. And she's making the most of it." Charlotte smiled. "But I think what she really enjoyed was hanging out with you for a day or two in the local jail."

Ray laughed. "Believe me, she didn't enjoy it, and neither did we."

"Still, with Brian back, we've now got two British stars. A real bonus for our patrons."

"And how will Audrey get along without Maxine?" Ray asked.

"Just fine. She was glad to see the back of her. There was a lot of tension between the two of them. It had been easy for Audrey to let Maxine take care of everything all those years, but I think she was ready for independence. To break free of that constant, overbearing presence."

Although who had left the cable for Mattie to trip over when she exited the stage during the dress rehearsal had not been determined, everyone had their suspicions. Ray had described the incident to the British authorities, who were now considering reopening the investigation into the accident that had led to the death of child star Gillian Pritchard.

"We'll see how it all works out, I guess," said Ray.

Charlotte began to relax and eventually wandered off to the newsstand to browse the magazines while Ray watched their belongings. Finally, their flight was called and boarding began. As they entered the aircraft and Charlotte turned to her right, the smiling flight attendant gently stopped her.

"Miss Fairfax."

"Yes?"

The flight attendant held out her right hand. "This way. You've been upgraded. You and Mr. Nicholson will be flying first class to London tonight."

Charlotte turned to Ray, who grinned at her. "You knew!" And after a moment, she let out a delighted laugh. "Paula!"

"I believe she made a phone call," Ray said. "She knows a lot of people in high places."

They took their seats, and Ray gently placed Charlotte's flight bag in the overhead bin. "It was really kind of you to offer to deliver Edmund's remains home to his family," he said. "I'm sure that means a lot to them."

Charlotte buckled her seat belt, sank into her seat, and turned to look at him.

"Happy?" she asked. He reached for her hand and nodded. Charlotte flipped through a magazine and sipped her glass of champagne as the flight crew prepared for departure. As the pushback began, the flight attendant collected Charlotte's empty glass, and they taxied into position for takeoff.

"And now," said Ray as they lifted off into the night sky and the twinkling lights of New York City disappeared below the clouds, "without further ado, let's get you home."

Acknowledgments

Thank you to Sheila Fletcher for her inspired and practical help at several stages of this book—especially the fun morning of devious plotting that set everything in motion.

I appreciate all the hard work by the terrific team at Crooked Lane Books: Matt Martz, who oversees everything; Sarah Poppe, for her brilliant editorial notes that reshaped the story; and Jenny Chen and the production people, who sorted out a problem or two.

And, as always, thanks to my agent, Dominick Abel, who brokers everything.